THIS BOOK BELONGS TO:

FREYA

DRUGAN. P6a

PRAISE FOR *THE CHRISTMAS CARROLLS*

'A Christmas book about kindness and cheer to make even Scrooge's heart melt.'
Dame Jacqueline Wilson

'This will put a smile on your face and a lump in your throat.'
Daily Mail

'Hilariously silly, this super-seasonal debut will have readers chuckling.'
Metro

'A beautifully written joyful story full of fun, friendship and the importance of kindness. Guaranteed to lift your spirits.'
A.F. Steadman, author of *Skandar and the Unicorn Thief*

'This book will fill your hearts and souls with joy, sparkle and most of all ho – ho – hope!'
Laura Ellen Anderson, author of Rainbow Grey and the bestselling Amelia Fang series

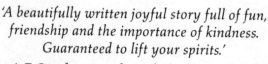

THE CHRISTMAS CARROLLS

THE CHRISTMAS COMPETITION

For
Felicity
X

First published in Great Britain 2022 by Farshore
An imprint of HarperCollins*Publishers*
1 London Bridge Street, London SE1 9GF

farshore.co.uk

HarperCollins*Publishers*
1st Floor, Watermarque Building, Ringsend Road
Dublin 4, Ireland

Text copyright © Mel Taylor-Bessent 2022
Illustration copyright © Selom Sunu 2022
The moral rights of the author and illustrator have been asserted.

ISBN 978 0 7555 0374 2
Signed edition ISBN 978 0 0085 9964 5

Printed and bound in the UK using 100% renewable electricity at CPI Group (UK) Ltd

1

A CIP catalogue record for this title is available from the British Library.

·THE·
CHRISTMAS
CARROLLS

THE CHRISTMAS COMPETITION

MEL TAYLOR-BESSENT

ILLUSTRATED BY SELOM SUNU

KHRIS

LAINA

THE KLAUSES

SUE

TOBOGGAN (Toby)

POINSETTIA (Setti)

HOLLY

NICK

THE CARROLLS

REGGIE

SNOW

IVY

RESCUING REGGIE

Have you ever woken up to the sound of sleigh bells, the smell of roasted chestnuts, and the feeling that your farting-wannabe-reindeer-donkey has crept out of your bed in the middle of the night?

You haven't? Well, count your lucky stars, my friends, because this was a morning like no other . . .

The air was crisp, the Christmas lights around my bed twinkled, and there was a giant, donkey-sized dent in my mattress.

"Reggie?" I said, scratching my head as I looked around my tinsel-covered bedroom. "Where are you?"

I slid off the bed, grabbed my snowman dressing gown, and checked all of his usual hiding places. He wasn't in my wardrobe, trying to squeeze himself into my favourite Christmas jumper. He wasn't in Mum and Dad's room, practising his breakdancing in front of their mirror. And he wasn't in the wrapping room, trying to make a secret den out of gift bags and wrapping paper.

Something didn't make sense. The only other place he'd go without me is . . .

"REGGIE!" Dad shouted from the front garden. "GET DOWN FROM THERE THIS INSTANT!"

My eyes grew as big as baubles. He wouldn't. Would he?

I ran on to the landing, hooked my leg over the banister and slid to the bottom of the stairs without a single bump, bruise or bumbling belly flop. I'd done it! I'd finally perfected my Mary Poppins bum slide! Ordinarily, I would bust out a celebratory dance, but Mum appeared at the front door carrying a trail of fairy lights, a long-handled duster and a look that was so shocked, you would've thought

Santa had just crash-landed in our garden.

"Holly, come quick!" she bawled. "It's a chrisaster! A CHRISASTER!"

I followed her into the front garden where Dad was pointing at something – or should I say someone – on the roof.

"Blinking baubles, Reg!" I cried. "How many times have I told you? You're not allowed up there!"

High on the tiles, Reggie stamped his hoof and glared at me with his non-wonky eye. "HEE-HAW!" he brayed.

"I know," I said, nodding like I understood. "And you *are* a reindeer if you want to be a reindeer, but you don't have your magic yet, remember? You haven't gone through reindeer school and you don't live at the North Pole and you won't be able to fly without –"

"HEE-HAW! HEE-HAW! HEE-HAW!"

"I *do* believe in you!" I said, trying my hardest to stay calm.

Reggie backed up as if preparing himself for a running jump.

"No!" Mum, Dad and I shouted together.

Reggie glowered and slumped back on his hind legs. He would've looked like one of those grumpy stone gargoyles on top of a church if it wasn't for his giant, inflatable antlers flapping in the wind.

"Pass me some tinsel, will you, Hols?" Mum said. She was holding a string of extra-long fairy lights and attaching one end to a wreath that Dad had squeezed over his hips. "Mission Rescue Reggie is a go!"

Now, I know what you're thinking. How can a wreath, some tinsel, and a whole load of fairy lights rescue a donkey on the roof? Normal decorations wouldn't be up to the task, of course, but these were Nick Carroll decorventions (decoration inventions), which meant they were made from the toughest materials, the strongest fibres and some clever Christmas concepts that Dad had spent years perfecting. Did you know his Toughened Tinsel was once used to pull a car out of a snowy ditch? And his Everlasting Fairy Lights can be stretched over a mile until they break?

Dad's pretty impressive when it comes to inventing things. I want to be just like him when I'm older. I also want to speak every language in the world, become Santa's Chief Wrapping Paper Designer, and learn how to deliver presents without using a chimney. But Mum said I need to finish school first. Spoilsport.

"Here Hols," Dad said, handing me my little sister. "Take care of Ivy while I climb on to the roof."

Ivy was wearing the same snowman dressing gown as me but with matching slippers and a snowflake hair clip that she kept trying to yank from her curls. She giggled as she waved her arms in the air and shouted, "Fly Weggie! Fly Weggie!"

With a running jump, Dad leaped on to my sleigh-shaped trampoline and launched himself halfway up the wall of the house. He looked like a giant ninja elf, complete with velvet pyjamas, a bell on the end of his hat, and stripy socks that covered his knees. I was thoroughly imprealous (when you're so impressed, you're jealous!) and I bet you would be, too, if you'd seen it.

Next, Dad scrambled up the decorventions that covered every inch of the house. There were extendable oven gloves that offered Christmas puddings on Christmas plates. There were mechanical stockings that swung back and forth and occasionally threw presents at passers-by. There were even carol-singing gingerbread men with moving arms and legs that helped give Dad the final push he needed to heave himself on to the roof.

It took a few minutes for Dad to shimmy past the life-size decorventions around the chimney, but when he reached Reggie, he fell to his knees and threw his arms around Reggie's neck.

"Don't scare us like that!" he said, stroking Reggie's head. "I know you're going to fly one day, but today's not the day, OK, boy?"

Reggie nuzzled his nose into Dad's belly and brayed

softly. As Dad led him to the edge of the roof, he hefted Reggie over his shoulders and used the Toughened Tinsel, Everlasting Fairy Lights and the wreath around his waist to make a DIY zip line. They whizzed down in a matter of seconds, but they didn't exactly nail the landing. *Oof.*

"Thank Santa you're OK," I said, snuggling into Reggie even though he let out a fart so stinky I threw up a little in my mouth.

"You gave us quite the scare!" Dad agreed.

"I think that's enough excitement for one day, don't you?" Mum said, leading us all back inside the house. "Why don't we make some hot chocolate and knit some stockings to calm our nerves?"

But that wasn't the end of the excitement. In fact, it was barely the beginning. Because what happened next was so baubilliant, so snow-tastic, so tinsel-riffic, it would blow the beard off Father Christmas himself . . .

THE LETTER

2

I hadn't had one sip of hot chocolate when the letter arrived. I was too busy busting a move with Ivy and Reggie because the postie had pressed the door bell that played *Jingle Bells* fourteen times in a row. The door bell dance-off had become a bit of a tradition, but I wasn't even halfway through my polar-bear prance when Dad came running into the room waving an envelope above his head.

"Code 9627!" he shouted. "CODE 9627!!!"

My head snapped up. Code 9627? *Again?*

"But Dad," I said, my hands frozen in the air like a polar bear getting its groove on. "Code 9627 is only used —"

"When something life changing or miraculous happens!" Mum cried. She chucked her knitting needles to one side and ran across the room so fast you would think she was powered by rocket fuel.

Dad waved the envelope. *The Christmas Chronicle* was stamped across the front and Dad had left sticky mince-pie fingerprints around the edges.

"There's a magazine inside," Dad said. "And this . . ." He jumped on to the sofa as if he was making a really important announcement and coughed three times before reading the letter out.

Dear Carroll family,

I don't know if you remember me. My name is Elton and I attended your big Christmas fundraiser last month. I came along with my wife and step-daughter, Alice, and I was blown away by your efforts to spread cheer to the rest of the community. Your Christmas spirit is infectious and I've been telling everyone I know about the family who celebrate Christmas every day of the year. My editor at *Newsflash* (the #1 selling newspaper in the country) was particularly keen to learn more about you because he also owns *The Christmas Chronicle* (a magazine I'm sure you've heard of already). This year, he's launching a new 'Most Festive Family' feature and he'll be scouring the country to find people that celebrate Christmas in the biggest way possible.

Dad stopped talking. His eyes whizzed across the rest of the page. His body went completely rigid.

"What is it, love?" Mum said.

"Dad!" I squealed, lifting Ivy on to my shoulders. "What's going on?"

"HEE-HAW! HEE-HAW!" Reggie bawled from across the room.

A bead of sweat had formed on Dad's head. His bottom lip quivered.

"Come on, Nick," Mum said, pulling her three-tiered snowflake hat away from her eyes. "You can't just –"

"STONKING STOCKINGS!" Dad cried. "ARE THEY SERIOUS?"

"What?" Mum said.

"What?" I yelled.

"Hee-haw! Hee-haw! Heeeee-haw!"

Waiting for Dad to talk again was like waiting for Santa to arrive on Christmas Eve. I even considered falling asleep in case that helped him tell us quicker.

"It's Elton," Dad stammered. "He's . . . he's already nominated us."

Mum and I looked at each other with wide eyes.

"And . . ." Dad added, ". . . we've been accepted."

"Snow way!" Mum gasped.

"Sleighriously?" I squealed.

Dad read the rest of the letter as quickly as he could. "Elton says they searched the entire country and found two families who 'excel at Christmas'."

"Just two families?" Mum said, her cheeks turning redder than Rudolph's nose. "Us and who else?"

"The Klauses," Dad said. "The Klauses of Candy

Cane Lane. All we have to do is prove that we're better at spreading cheer and we'll be named the Most Festive Family in the entire country!"

Mum looked like all of her Christmases had come at once. She began jumping up and down, tiny flecks of fake snow fluttering down from her snowflake hat.

"And then what?" she squealed. "Do we get a certificate? Will they use us as an example for the rest of the world to spread cheer, too?"

Dad shook his head with a grin. "The winning family get an all-expenses paid trip to New York City."

"NEW YORK CITY!"

"Next month."

"NEXT MONTH??"

"Where they'll appear on the leading float in the Christmas Season Parade."

Mum stared at Dad with bulging eyes. "Christmas. Season. Par–"

"Wait," Dad said, turning the letter over. "That's not all."

The fire crackled and hissed. The *Jingle Bells* door bell stopped ringing. Reggie stopped scratching his bum on the sofa.

"The Editor of *The Christmas Chronicle* wants to witness our Christmas festivities for himself," Dad whispered. "He wants to come here. To Sleigh Ride Avenue. On the twenty-third of October. He wants us to pretend it's Christmas Day so a photographer can take photos for the magazine and he can see the different things we do to celebrate."

"So it's like a Christmas rehearsal?" Mum said, clutching Dad's hand to steady herself.

Dad nodded. "And we have exactly two weeks until he arrives."

Mum fell into a trance. Dad stared at the letter. Reggie let out an excited fart. (Er, OK, maybe that wasn't Reggie.)

"CHRISTMAS STATIONS!" Dad roared, running out of the room in his elf pyjamas.

"TO THE WORKSHOP!" Mum yelled, tossing her hat in the air and racing after him.

"HEE-HAAAAW!" Reggie cried, bounding after them both.

Ivy clapped her hands and giggled with excitement on my shoulders. "Klauses," she said. "Klauses more Christmas."

I frowned.

Was Ivy right? We didn't know anything about the Klauses, but they couldn't be more festive than us. Could they?

OUT-CHRISTMASSED

3

W e spent the rest of the weekend rushing around the house like frantic elves on Christmas Eve. There was a SANTA'S SACKLOAD of work to do. Reggie spent his time practising his wonky pout and wobbly poses for the photographer, while Mum, Dad and I worked harder than we ever had before (yep, even harder than that time Dad tried to run a marathon wearing his entire Christmas jumper collection and we had to drag him home on my toy sleigh).

Complete with Santa hats, red felt aprons and half-moon glasses, we raced from Dad's workshop to the wrapping room, from the kitchen to the reindeer stables, and by sunset on Sunday, we ended up in Mum's apron studio hidden under piles of fake fur, crushed velvet and fairy lights.

"OK, family," Dad yawned as he pulled the curtains shut. "What's our cheer-o-meter ratings for today?"

Mum lifted a sleeping Ivy on to her shoulder. "Mine's got to be a ten out of ten," she said, motioning towards her sewing table. "The editor from *The Christmas Chronicle* will get his choice of festive attire as soon as he walks through the door. I've made him a snowtacular fluffy jumper, complete with bells on the cuffs and three layers of tinsel around the collar. I've also made him a limited edition Snow Carroll apron that says 'There's snow Christmas like Christmas with the Carrolls!'. AND a bobble hat that plays *We Wish You A Merry Christmas* every hour, on the hour."

"Wow, Mum!" I beamed. "If I were him, I'd explite" – that means explode with excitement by the way – "as soon as I arrived!"

"Speaking of explitements," Dad said, wiggling his eyebrows up and down, "I've finally cracked those Christmas fireworks I've been trying to make for years."

"The ones that can fit inside a Christmas cracker?" I cried, feeling like I might actually explite myself any second.

Dad nodded proudly. "And I'm working on that rotating bauble organiser I told you about last week. If we're going to win this competition, we need to show the editor just how inventive we are!"

"Absnowlutely," Mum said, keeping her voice down so she didn't wake Ivy. "What about you, Snowdrop? What's your cheer-o-meter rating for the day?"

I smiled nervously. "Er . . ."

Helping Mum and Dad? Ten out of ten. Making a new type of tinsel from torn newspaper, environmentally friendly glitter and old shoelaces? Eight out of ten.

Missing Alice's birthday party? Zero out of ten.

"I think we've all out-Christmassed ourselves," I said eventually. "And you can't put a number on that."

"Well said!" Dad chuckled, grabbing the last snowberry pie from the plate and turning off the lights on Christmas tree number twenty-two.

Phew. The last time I'd said out loud that my cheer-o-meter rating was less than nine and a half, they'd almost fainted.

"Well then," Mum said, following Dad out of her studio. "What's on the ice-tinerary tomorrow?"

Dad muttered something about waffles and snow syrup for breakfast, then kissed Mum's forehead and sprinted into the kitchen for some late-night bakeventions (baking inventions).

I sat in the dark a moment longer. Mum and Dad were undubidedly two of the most joyful people on the planet. It was like the magic of Christmas ran in their veins. Spreading cheer came as naturally to them as breathing.

I used to be the same, I suppose. But things felt different now. Not good different or bad different. Just . . . *strange* different.

Like today, when I was supposed to be concentrating on my plastic-free tinsel but dreaming of being at Alice's party instead. Or like the other night when we were eating our bazillionth Christmas dinner and all I could think about was the pizza and chips my friends had every Friday night.

I guess I'd been daydreaming a lot lately. Dreaming of skateboarding in the park, trips to the seaside and wearing clothes that weren't red or green.

It's not that I didn't enjoy looking after the reindeer, decorating our forty-five Christmas trees or singing carols every morning. But sometimes I wondered if I could just, I don't know . . . have a day off?

THE OPPOSITE OF SPREADING CHEER

4

Dad played the Christmas car playlist twice as loud to keep him awake the following morning. He said he'd been up all night trialling different types of bread to offer the editor of *The Christmas Chronicle*: apple and cinnamon, cranberry and orange, toasted honey and almond, and my personal favourite, gumdrop fruitcake. Apparently he'd done thirty-two taste tests, broken two bowls, trapped his finger in the cookie jar and taken the leftover bread to the local food bank before Mum and I had sung our first carol of the day. He was so elf-ficient.

"So, Snowflake," he said, passing me my Backpack of Cheer as I climbed out of the car. "Are you still OK to give Reggie a bath later?"

I groaned. I thought ~~Mum~~ and Dad had forgotten about Reggie's matted fur and stinky ~~armpits~~ legpits.

"As long as he promises not to headbutt me this time," I replied. "That bruise has only just faded."

Dad gave me a thumbs up and tooted the *Jingle Bells* car horn. "Have fun today, Snowflake. Remember to spread cheer wherever you go!"

I skipped through the school gates and waved back at him. "Bye, Dad! Remember to spread cheer with a ho, ho –"

Oh.

I blinked once. Twice. Three times.

"WHAT IN SANTA'S NAME IS THIS?" I screeched.

The sound of *Driving Home for Christmas* and Dad's rusty exhaust had been replaced by children squealing 'Happy Halloween!' and Mrs Spencer, the head teacher, wishing them a 'spooktacular day' as they walked past her office. She'd placed a speaker on a table that filled the corridor with the gloomy sound of organ pipes and even decorated her door with cotton-wool cobwebs and plastic spiders.

"What's going on?" I said, finding Alice and Liena in the library beside the 'horror' section. They were wearing long purple wigs under pointy hats and they'd made themselves badges that said *Chief Event Organisers.*

"It's the Halloween Haunt!" Liena said, shoving a clipboard and pen under my nose. "You are coming, aren't you? It's in two weeks. Make sure you write down what costume you're going to wear so that nobody wears the same thing."

I gulped. Halloween? Wasn't that a day for scaring people and throwing eggs at houses and doing everything you could *not* to spread cheer? I'd heard about it once, way before we moved to Sleigh Ride Avenue and I started at Lockerton Primary School. Mum and Dad were talking about poor Mrs Ovi who had her car tyres slashed in a Halloween prank so she couldn't drive to work. And then there was Mr Turner who had to close his shop early every Halloween because some pranksters were trying to scare his customers. Mum even said that there are some Halloween movies that give people nightmares and I overheard Dad say that he's hated Halloween ever since his siblings hid a tarantula under his pillow.

"It's going to be the scariest event ever!" Yolandé shouted, making me jump.

"Mrs Spencer said we can tell ghost stories around a campfire!" Lauren said.

"And there's going to be a disco with spooky music," Marie added.

I shivered. Spooky music? Ghost stories? Scariest event ever? They were all talking as if Halloween was supposed to be . . . *fun?*

"I bet you'll win the dance-off," Shelley said to Marie, who was twirling around the library in a rubber zombie mask. "Are you making your own costume this year, Soph?"

Sophie nodded. "I've been thinking about being a

cavegirl or a cat. Or I might make a mummy costume out of bandages like I did last year."

I looked at my classmates one at a time. Surely they were joking? Yes, that had to be it. Only two weeks ago, they were telling me how much they enjoyed spreading cheer every day. They couldn't have forgotten already.

"Ha ha! Very funny," I said, looking around for hidden cameras. "You can stop pretending now."

"Hey!" a voice yelled from the other side of the library. "The posters turned out great! What shall we make next?"

I recognised the voice.

"Archer?" I cried, making room for him around the table. "Don't tell me you like Halloween, too?"

Archer grabbed the clipboard to add his costume to the list and grinned. "Of course," he said. "What's not to love about scaring people?"

"Didn't you know Archie loves Halloween?" Alice said, giving Archer a pile of posters to hand out. "I thought you two were best buds?"

I gulped. We *were* best buds. We'd been best buds for all of four and a half weeks, and that basically meant we knew everything about each other. Didn't it?

I looked Archer up and down, wondering how I hadn't seen this side of him before. He'd always been so kind and caring. He loves animals (especially Reggie!) and he was the only one who helped me when I joined Lockerton Primary School and felt like the odd one out. How could someone like that also enjoy something as frightening as Halloween? And did that mean I was supposed to like it, too? The very thought made me want to throw up.

No. There's a reason us Carrolls try to spread cheer all year and it's because people want to be happy, not frightened!

"YOU like Halloween?" I said, not bothering to hide my disgustament (when you're disgusted and disappointed at the same time).

"Er, yes," Archer said meekly.

"But . . . *why*?"

Archer shuffled his feet. "I've always helped arrange the Halloween Haunt. We would've asked you to join us, but you've been a bit, er . . ."

"Cheerful?" I said. "Happy? Not at all scary?"

"Distracted," Alice and Liena said together.

I stared at them with wide eyes. The other Year Five girls backed away.

"They mean *dedicated*," Archer said, resting his hand on my arm. "Dedicated to spreading cheer."

"You say that like it's a bad thing," I said.

"Being dedicated isn't bad," Archer said in a soft tone. "But you could make time for other things, too. You know, step outside your comfort zone?"

"I do step outside my comfort zone!" I said, feeling my cheer-o-meter rating nose-dive to a weak five and a half. "The other day I decorated half a Christmas tree and turned the empty side round so no one would see. Can you imagine that? Only decorating HALF a tree? I lost sleep over it for three whole nights. That didn't feel comfortable at all."

"I mean *really* step out of your comfort zone," Archer said, trying not to laugh. "Like doing something that scares you. Or doing something you've never done before."

I frowned. "Like dressing up for Halloween and going to a scary party?"

"Sure," Archer shrugged, handing me a poster. "It's a start."

I looked at the poster warily. I mean, yes, I'd been

craving some time away from Christmas duties. And yes, I'd been dreaming about spending one weekend doing something other than ice-skating and present wrapping. But a Halloween party? That felt like a hundred steps too far.

"Holly?" Alice said, waving her clipboard in front of me. "Will you be there?"

"I don't know," I admitted. "Can I think about it?"

THE SCARIEST THING I CAN THINK OF

5

Cobweb-covered thoughts haunted my mind for the rest of the day. What sort of costume did you wear to a Halloween party? Would they expect me to scare people for fun? And what would Mum and Dad say if I agreed to celebrate the one event they despised?

I hugged my Backpack of Cheer a little tighter and pulled my Hollyhood around me. It smelled of snow-covered fir trees, cinnamon and crispy roast potatoes. Although that would normally have helped me relax, all I could think about was what *Halloween* smelled like. Dead bodies, decay, rotting wood, murky water . . .

"Holly?" Miss Eversley said.

"EYEBALLS!" I shouted.

A wave of laughter rippled across the room.

I blushed. "I mean . . . yes, Miss Eversley?"

"It's your turn to read your poem," Miss Eversley said, shaking her head as if I'd made her wait all day to open her Christmas presents. "Your Halloween poem?"

I scrambled up from my table and walked to the front of the room.

"The Scariest Things I Can Think Of," I said, reading the title of my Halloween poem as clearly as I could. "The world running out of candy canes, white chocolate and chicken gravy. Getting coal in my stocking. Not winning the Most Festive Family competition. Forgetting to sing my morning carols. Christmas being cancelled. Halloween. Disappointing my parents. Not making friends. And . . ." My voice trembled. "Losing my cheer."

I could hardly look up. I wasn't used to talking about or even *thinking* about my fears. Where was the cheer in that? Archer clapped quietly and the rest of the class followed as I walked back to my seat with my head down.

"Thank you, Holly," Miss Eversley said. "Isn't it interesting how different our fears are? From global warming to running out of candy canes, all of our fears are valid and we should try very hard to understand each other and appreciate that we are all unique."

Dan and Arun were the next to read their poem about the scariest things they could think of. They talked about animals becoming extinct and natural disasters like floods and fires and droughts. They mentioned trees being cut down in the rainforests and the oceans being filled with plastic. When they finished, the whole class cheered and Miss Eversley gave them three gold stars. EACH!

Ordinarily I'd have been super jealous, but they had a point. Plastic filling the ocean was far scarier than coal in my stocking, and animals becoming extinct was more important than the world running out of candy canes. Maybe if I thought a little less about Christmas, my brain would have room to think about things like that? Maybe if I spread a little less cheer, I'd realise that there were bigger problems in the world?

"Holly?" Alice said, waving her hand in front of my face. "Are you coming?"

I shook myself from my trance. When had the bell gone?

"Coming where?" I said, slinging my Backpack of Cheer over my shoulder.

"To my house." Alice smiled, linking arms with Liena. "To make masks for the Halloween Haunt?"

My heart wanted to jump for joy. I'd been waiting for weeks for someone to invite me to their house, but this invite came with conditions. I could only go to Alice's house if I made a scary mask. I could only go to Alice's house if I acted as though I liked Halloween. I could only go to Alice's house if I forgot everything I believed in.

"I can't," I said, feeling a teensy bit relieved. "I have to give my donkey a bath."

Alice smiled like she wasn't sure if I was joking or not.

"Can't you do that tomorrow?" Liena asked.

I shook my head. "Tomorrow I need to design Christmas dinner menus and taste-test Dad's new Festiwater. It's his latest invention where he mixes Christmas flavours with water. He wants to bottle it up and give the money it makes to charity."

"What about this weekend?" Alice said. "Can't you give Reggie a bath then?"

That might've been a good idea if I hadn't had a never-ending list of things to do before the editor of *The Christmas Chronicle* came.

"When exactly *is* the Halloween Haunt?" I said, air quoting 'Halloween Haunt' like it was all just a big joke.

"The twenty-third of October," Alice said. "Just before the half -term break."

Why did that date sound so familiar? My mind raced to the note Elton sent us. Of course! It was the same day the editor of *The Christmas Chronicle* was coming to visit. Would I be able to squeeze both into one day?

And more importantly, did I want to?

"This weekend we're making Christmas crackers and decorating a new tree in the dining room," I said, already feeling calmer at the thought of so much festiveness. "And I'm helping Dad re-ice the ice rink and Mum's asked me to make her hair whiter."

"It's OK, Holly," Alice said, walking out of the door with Liena. "Maybe next time."

I pulled my Hollyhood around my ears and sighed. Would I rather go to Alice's house than give Reggie a bath and get kicked in the head when he got water in his eyes? Probably. Would Mum and Dad let me make Halloween masks instead of prepare for the biggest Christmas rehearsal of their life? Never in a million years.

BUBBLE BEARDS

6

An hour later, I was balancing on the edge of the bath with a very wet, very smelly, very *grumpy* donkey looking up at me. In typical Reggie style, he'd refused to take his inflatable antlers off, and they kept hitting the shower hose and spraying water across the room. Within five minutes I was drenched from head to toe, and everything from the carol-singing toilet seat and Toyland tiles were covered in water and Reggie's grey hairs.

"Hello?" a voice called from the hallway.

"ARCHER!" I cried.

"HEE-HAW!" Reggie bawled.

"Alice told me you were bathing Reggie tonight," Archer said, pushing the bathroom door open. "I thought you might need a helping hand?"

As soon as Reggie spotted Archer, he leaped up, thrashing his head from left to right. He got so excited that his hooves hit the candy-cane taps, and green and red water sloshed into the already overflowing bath.

"Archer!" I shrieked, getting squished against the tiles by Reggie's enormous bum. "Turn the taps off! Turn the taps off!"

Archer somehow turned the taps off while repositioning Reggie and stroking his head enough to calm him. Reggie nuzzled into Archer's armpit and brayed softly.

"He hates this!" I muttered, scrubbing Reggie's back slowly so I didn't startle him. "But I'm the only one he'll let bathe him. He won't even let Dad go near him with a watering can!"

Archer washed behind Reggie's ears. "So why are you doing this if he hates being cleaned so much?"

"Shivering snowballs!" I gasped. "I haven't told you!"

"About what?"

I dropped the sponge and Dad's special bubble mixture into the water. "The editor. New York. The most festive family. The Christmas rehearsal."

Archer looked at me like I was speaking donkey language.

"The Klauses of Candy Cane Lane!" I cried. "*The Christmas Chronicle*. Two weeks. We can't be out-Christmassed!"

Archer wrestled with Reggie's inflatable antlers so he could see me properly. "You're not making sense," he said. "Take a deep breath and tell me everything."

Five minutes later, I'd filled Archer in about *The Christmas Chronicle*, the 'Most Festive Family' feature, and all the things we were going to do to win.

"That's brilliant!" Archer said, scrubbing the last of the dirt from Reggie's hooves. "Why didn't you tell me earlier?"

"I sort of . . . *forgot*," I said, shocking myself as I

said the words out loud.

"Holly Carroll? Forget about Christmas? I don't think so!" Archer teased.

"Everyone was too busy talking about the Halloween Haunt," I said, already craving a pinecone pie or snowball sundae to lift my Christmas spirit. "My parents have always said how terrible Halloween is, but it's all anyone at school could talk about. Even you."

Archer bit his lip like he was afraid to say something that might offend me. "You know I love Christmas," he said. "But I love Halloween, too. It's a bit like enjoying a vanilla milkshake *and* a hot chocolate. They're total opposites, but you can still like both."

Milkshakes and hot chocolate were worlds apart from spreading cheer and spreading fear, but I sort of saw where he was coming from. Maybe it was OK to like different things. Sometimes?

"I'm sorry, Arch," I said, now craving a giant hot-chocolate-flavoured milkshake. "I really don't think Halloween is for me. I'm all for trying something new and I'd *love* to do something that isn't always related to Christmas, but maybe not the Halloween Haunt. Besides, I wouldn't know what to go as."

Suddenly, Archer and Reggie started to laugh. At first I thought they were laughing at me, but when Reggie's laugh turned into a grunting hiccup and he let out one of his stinky, lingering farts, I knew he was excited about something.

"What?" I said. "What are you laughing at?"

"I think Reggie's found a costume for you, Hols," Archer chuckled.

"How?" I said. "He's been sitting in the bath the entire . . . oh."

As if he was in one of those fancy shampoo adverts on TV, Reggie tossed his mane to one side and sent water droplets flying in all directions. Turning to look at me in slow motion, he raised his eyebrows, spread his wonky smile as wide as he could and showed off the most snowtacular beard of bubbles I'd ever seen.

"Father Christmas?" I gasped, tears of laughter

streaming down my face. "You think I should go as Father Christmas to the Halloween Haunt?"

My mind danced with the idea of bringing a little festiveness to the Halloween Haunt. Could I go as a half-eaten candy cane? A melting snowman? A child with a lump of coal in their stocking? I shivered. Even that seemed like a step too far.

Reggie seemed to wink. Then Archer and I scooped bubbles into our hands and made our own bubble beards. We laughed wildly as I grabbed my half-moon glasses and my Hollyhood from the back of the bathroom door and Archer flicked the festadio on in the corner.

And that was how we spent the rest of the evening – singing along to Christmas songs, dressed as bubbly Father Christmases, and trying not to get dragged into the bath with a farting donkey and his inflatable antlers. It was one of the best evenings I'd had in ages, until . . .

THE FINALISTS

7

"Mrs Carroll?" Archer said, turning the volume on the festadio down. "Are you feeling OK?"

Mum had appeared in the open doorway, her hands shaking and her cheeks pale.

"What's happened?" I said. "Do you need to sit down?"

Mum's bottom lip quivered. "They've revealed the finalists for the Most Festive Family competition," she said. "There's a whole article. On the Internet. And . . . and . . ."

"Oh no," I said. "Have they spelt our surname wrong?"

Mum shook her head, making the bells in her hair jingle.

"Have they used an unflattering photo?"

Mum shook her head harder.

"Have they revealed that your real name isn't actually Snow?" I said, coaxing Reggie out of the bath with a handful of candy canes.

Mum's eyes filled with tears. "It's the Klauses," she managed to say.

"The other family?" Archer said, chucking a towel over Reggie's head and patting his neck dry.

Mum nodded. "They're . . . they're . . ." Her voice became so high-pitched, I'm surprised it didn't shatter all the windows in the house. "They're the most Christmassy family I've ever seen!" she cried.

Five minutes later, we were crowded around Dad's laptop in the kitchen. Dad was reading the article for what must have been the bazillionth time, staring at the screen with wide eyes and stirring his brownie mixture so hard it had turned to a gloopy lumpy

mess that looked a bit like Reggie's –

"TWO!" Dad bawled, smearing sticky chocolate across the computer screen. "They have TWO life-size sleighs on the roof. Look, Snow. Can you see?"

Mum grabbed hold of Archer to keep her upright.

"The article says they have *two hundred and fifty* Christmas trees," Dad continued. "And an Ice Kingdom, whatever that is. They dine with royalty on Boxing Day AND they own their own winter village in Lapland."

"Who *are* these people?" Archer breathed. "They're like you but more . . ."

Dad and I looked at him. Mum whimpered. Reggie let out a nervous fart.

"Christmas!" Ivy yelled from her cot upstairs. "MORE CHRISTMAAAAAS!"

Archer's cheeks flushed pink.

"Maybe they're not 'more Christmas'," I said hopefully. I looked at Dad's *Head Elf* apron, Mum's jingly dress and our kitchen overflowing with tinsel and fairy lights and shelves crammed with festive teapots. "Maybe they just said all those things to win the competition. Maybe they don't have any of that at all?"

Dad's glazed eyes began sparkling again. "That's it!" he said. "We need to see it for ourselves."

"We do?"

"Holly, you're a genius!" Dad beamed, picking me up and twirling me around the kitchen. "We'll go tonight."

"Tonight?" Mum and I cried.

"Ivy can sleep in the car," Dad said, rummaging in cupboards and pulling a batch of sweet-smelling mince pies from the oven. "We don't have to go *in*, of course. We'll just see if they've got two sleighs on the roof. We'll drive past and see if this so-called Ice Kingdom is real. We'll poke our heads over the fence and see if they really do have two hundred and fifty Christmas trees."

"Isn't it getting a little late, love?" Mum said, checking the new ho-ho clock on the wall. (It used to be a cuckoo clock until Dad replaced the bird with a bell-ringing Santa.)

"Not at all," Dad cried, pouring hot chocolate into a giant snowman flask. "Just think of it as a little road trip. We'll practise some carols, eat the leftover snowiches from lunch, and come straight back. What do you say? You're coming, too, aren't you, Archer?"

Archer shoved his hands in his pockets. "I'm sorry,

Mr Carroll. I have to go," he said, shuffling his feet from side to side. "I promised Alice I'd help make masks for the Halloween Haunt."

"You're still going to that?" I said, holding my arms out so Dad could pile them with blankets, binoculars and a blizzard emergency kit: you know, all the travel essentials.

"Just for a bit," Archer said. "I did promise."

I looked at the floor. If Archer and everyone at school enjoyed Halloween, was there a tiny chance that I could, too? It was just some mask making. I could always include some glitter or baubles or twinkling fairy lights to make them less scary. Or just use it as an excuse to spend time with my friends.

Was Halloween as bad as Mum and Dad made it out to be?

A BIG FAT LIE

8

"REGGIE CARROLL!" Mum shrieked.

Reggie had leaped into the boot of the car just as Mum finished filling it up with stacks of stripy stockings and sweet treats.

"There's no room for you, Reginald," Mum cried, dragging him out of the car and round the side of the house. "Go to your stables like a good don– I mean, *reindeer* – and you can have *two* breakfasts in the morning. How does that sound?"

Reggie dragged his hooves across the grass and kicked dirt up the back of his freshly washed legs. Then he hung his head to one side and let out a soft, lonely hee-haw.

"I'm sorry, boy," I shouted after him. "We'll –"

But he had already stomped off, swaying his bum from side to side like an angry model on a catwalk.

"Come on!" Dad yelled, honking the *Jingle Bells* car horn. "My map of Santa Shortcuts says that Candy Cane Lane is over an hour away. We'd better get our ice skates on."

As Reggie clomped towards the stables, I turned to face the car.

"Where have the antlers gone?" I said, blinking hard to check I wasn't seeing things. "And the fur from the bonnet? The red nose on the bumper? The sleigh on the roof rack? What have you done with it all?"

"We need to be inconspicuous," Dad said, revving the engine.

"In-con-what?" I asked.

"It means he wants to go unnoticed," Mum explained as I hopped into the back seat. "We don't want to draw any attention to ourselves." She squeezed into the passenger seat and almost took up the entire car with her frilly dress and dangling bells.

"Sure," I said, smiling at Dad's elf apron with matching hat, stripy socks and curly-toed shoes. "Because we don't stand out at all!"

As soon as we pulled out of the drive, it felt like Halloween was haunting me. Our neighbour had put a giant pumpkin in the window of their house with the outline of a cat carved into it. Another house had a whole row of pumpkins leading to their front door and others had some dotted around their gardens. A few pumpkins had been painted white, covered in glitter, and had glowing candles inside. They actually looked quite nice, but I was way too afraid to say that out loud. Mum and Dad were upset enough about the Klauses and the Most Festive Family competition without having to worry about me sort of, kind of, a teeny tiny bit coming around to the idea of pretty pumpkins and Halloween parties.

While Mum sketched a new apron design and Dad shouted 'Merry Christmas!' to every driver on the road,

I spent the journey counting pumpkins. By the time I reached one hundred and fifty-six, I'd lost count, the sun had set, and the car had slowed to a crawl.

"This can't be right," Dad said, checking his map of Santa Shortcuts. "This can't be right at all."

I squished my face against the glass on the window and blinked like I didn't believe what my eyes were showing me.

NO WAY!

THIS was Candy Cane Lane?

The giant 'Welcome to Candy Cane Lane' sign looked like it was made from real candy canes. Dad pulled up to a barrier that had been wrapped with silver and red tinsel.

"Why would you have a barrier to keep people out?" Mum said, poking her head out of the window. "That doesn't spread cheer at all."

Beside the barrier, a man wearing a long candy cane coat and matching hat poked his head out of a stripy red and white booth that was filled with TV screens and security cameras.

"Keep going!" he yelled, his giant hat slipping over his eyes so all we could see was his beaming smile and bushy moustache. "The light team have your passes. They've have been waiting for you!"

"Light team?" Dad said, his eyebrows furrowing.

"Park up in the service entrance," the man said, raising the barrier. "But for heaven's sake, don't let Mr and Mrs Klaus see you. They don't appreciate tardiness."

"Fartyness?" I said. "It's a good job we didn't bring Reggie then!"

Mum giggled and made the bells in her hair tinkle. "*Tardiness* means being late, Holly," she said.

I made a mental note to add my new favourite word to my Holly Carroll Dictionary. It would say something like: *Fartyness: when a fart slips out later than expected.*

"I think you're mistaken, sir," Dad said, stepping out of the car. "We're –"

"Oh good. They sent your uniforms in advance," the security ~~officer~~ elf-ficer said, looking at Dad's elf apron and frilly socks. "Just follow the road around the bend and you'll find the service entrance on your left. If you get as far as the snow fountains, you've gone too far."

I was sure that Dad would elf-splain that the man had got it all wrong. He would give the elf-cuse that we'd taken a wrong turn, that we'd never meant to come to Candy Cane Lane. He would elf– er . . . I ran out of elf-deas.

But NO. Dad had to do the one thing that was worse than celebrating Halloween.

He lied.

"Yes, yes, yes. We've been here before," he said, trying his best to look cool and calm but tripping over his own feet and almost landing face first on the pavement. "It's going to be a long shift, I think!"

The security elf-ficer's beaming smile wavered. "Just remember to be gone by sunrise. The Klauses like their workforce to slip in and out unseen. Like Father Christmas."

Dad gave an awkward salute and then stumbled back into the car.

"Nicholas!" Mum cried, gathering up her layers of skirt so Dad could drive without tons of tulle and tinsel in his way. "What are you doing?"

"We didn't come all this way just to chat to the security guard," Dad said, putting the car into gear and pulling forward. "Have you seen what they've got, Snow? Candy Cane Lane isn't a row of houses. It's *one* house. *Their* house. The Klauses own ALL of Candy Cane Lane. And we have to see it if we've got any chance of beating them."

"But we're trespassing!" Mum said, her hands beginning to shake. "We'll be on the naughty list. You've got to stop, Nick."

"We'll just do what the security guard told us," Dad said, his eyes firmly fixed on the road. "There's a service entrance for the workers. We'll use that and –"

Dad stopped. Mum gasped. Ivy woke from her sleep and let out a quiet 'Ooooh.'

"This isn't good," I said, waiting for the car to roll to a stop. "This isn't good at all."

CANDY CANE LANE

9

The lane in front of us widened. Tall fir trees reached high into the sky on either side, and workers dressed in elaborate elf costumes were climbing up and down ladders and adding fairy lights to the branches.

"Not too close!" one elf worker shouted to another. "The lights need to be five centimetres apart, remember? Not a millimetre over or a millimetre under. The Klauses were very particular about that."

Struggling under the weight of the lights, another elf worker sighed. "But there are hundreds of trees!" she groaned. "Do they really expect us to get it all done tonight?"

Dad moved the car forward so we didn't look too sasspicious. All around us, trees twinkled like disco balls, and silver tinsel snaked around the tree trunks. Even the concrete road had been replaced with mirrored tiles, so the lights and tinsel reflected in the road surface and made it look like we were driving through starlight. Above our heads, giant, light-up angels spread from one side of the road to the other. They hung from the tips of trees by invisible wire and moved so gently in the wind, it looked like they were flying.

"Dad," I whispered, my insides feeling heavier than a ball of ice. "Mum's right. I'm not sure we should be here."

"Not you, too, Snowflake," Dad said, speeding up a little. "Don't you want to be named the Most Festive Family?"

I looked out of the window and gulped. "Well, yes, but –"

"Then we need to see the competition," Dad declared. "We need to see if we need more lights or more snow or more tushy tinsel toilet paper."

Dad shot past the service entrance and around another bend.

And that was when we saw it.

The house.

The house on Candy Cane Lane.

The house that would undubidedly win the Most Festive Family award.

"Christmas!" Ivy giggled, taking in the snow fountains, ice bridges and giant silver candy canes that spread out before us. "More Christmas!"

Dad skidded the car to a stop. The house that stood behind the fountains and bridges and billion glowing candy canes wasn't an ordinary house. In fact, it looked like three enormous houses stuck together. Tall turrets stood at either end, and the whole house had been painted such a bright white, it looked like it had been covered in whipped cream and icing sugar.

"That's it," Mum said, her eyes filling with tears. "They've already won."

Dad opened his mouth to reply, but nothing came out.

Mum had a point. The Klauses' house was perfectly symmetrical, with huge arched windows, double doors with reindeer-head knockers, and bright white lights cascading down the walls. It glowed so much, it might as well have been made from diamonds.

"I think we should leave," I said, wishing I had the Christmacam with me to take a photo. "I have homework to do and Reggie is probably missing us and Archer might be calling me to help with his Halloween mask."

"I think you're right," Dad said, finally seeing the light – or a bazillion lights, in this case. He put the car into reverse and quietly turned us around.

Before I knew what was happening, blinding floodlights burst into life from the top of the two turrets and trapped us in a yellowy glow. Then the song *Step Into Christmas* blasted out of speakers hidden inside the fountains, and snow catapulted into the air from the top of the ice bridges.

"We've been spotted!" Mum cried, nervously playing

with the bells in her hair. "Quick, Nick. Put your foot down. *Put your foot down!*"

"Too late," Dad whispered as the front doors of the house opened. "Here come the Klauses."

Four figures with perfect postures glided out of the double doors. They all wore matching velvet coats with enormous, fur-lined hoods and perma-smiles stretched across their faces.

"Welcome!" the lady sang, sashaying past the reindeer-shaped trees with her arms stretched wide and her red velvet cloak billowing behind her. "You must be the Carrolls?"

I couldn't help gawping at them. Even the two children didn't have a hair out of place.

"PRESENTING . . ." a loud voice boomed across the speakers that were hidden inside the fountains, "MR KLAUS."

Mr Klaus bowed and wrapped his arm around his wife.

"MRS KLAUS," the voice continued.

Mrs Klaus drew her thin red lips into a pout and curtseyed.

"MASTER KLAUS."

A boy about my age straightened his back even more and stuck his nose in the air.

"AND MISS KLAUS," the voice finished.

The girl (who looked almost identical to her brother) held her cloak out an at angle and stared into the distance like an ~~elefant~~ elegant ballerina.

"Are these people actually related to Santa?" I whispered.

Mum let out a little groan. Ivy blew a raspberry. Dad's eyes practically fell from their sockets.

"What do we do?" I said, prodding Mum's shoulder. "Run? Hide? Wait for Santa to save us?"

"I wouldn't advise that," a stern voice said. "The Klauses don't like to be kept waiting."

For a moment I thought someone was speaking through the fountain speakers, but the voice was too quiet, too near, too –

A hand tapped on the car window.

"OHHH!" Mum cried, jumping in her seat.

"SLUSHY SNOWFLAKES!" Dad yelled, pressing his hand to his heart.

"ARRRGHHH!" I yelled.

"Elf!" squeaked Ivy.

She clapped her hands as a tall, thin man in an elf hat peered through the car window.

"Please, come with me," he said dully. "And don't be

too cheerful. The Klauses won't like feeling out-cheered in their own home and you have *quite* the reputation."

"A reputation?" I said, craning my neck to see just how tall this so-called elf was. "For being cheerful? Wait – we have a cheerutation?" I rummaged in my Backpack of Cheer, wondering whether I could make some *Cheerutation* badges out of my school reading journal, a pot of red glitter and some old rubber bands.

"Please," the elf said, tapping his foot. "Allow me to introduce you to the Klauses and then you can be on your way."

Dad looked at Mum nervously. "I don't think we have much choice," he said. "At least we didn't come all this way for nothing."

"Let's just be ourselves," Mum said with a smile, squeezing Dad's hand. "The Klauses love Christmas just as much as we do. I'm sure we'll get along famously."

"You're right," Dad said, stepping out of the car and brushing some crumbs from his elf apron. "Come on, Carrolls. Let's spread cheer wherever we go . . ."

Mum and I jumped out of the car and did a little jig. "Let's spread cheer with a ho-ho –"

"NO!" the elf said, wagging his finger at us. "No, no,

     no,

          no,

               no,

          no,

NO.

          I said no cheer, remember?"

A
FROSTY ⑩
WELCOME

"The trick to walking on the ice is to stay flat-footed," the elf explained. "Right foot – slide. Left foot – slide. Right foot –"

SPLAT.

Just as I was doing my third right-foot slide, my Hollyhood caught under my shoe and sent my legs flying into the air. Seconds later, I crashed on to the mirrored ground and heard it *crack*. Although my Backpack of Cheer softened the fall, I whizzed across the ice and hurtled bum first into Mum and Ivy, who fell into Dad, who toppled on to the tall elf, who yelled out something like, *"Hi poo I poo fizz fob!"* (Actually it *might* have been 'Why do I do this job?' but a poo fizz fob sounds much more exciting.) Like a snowball gaining momentum in an avalanche, we rolled across the ice in a tangle of arms, legs and jingling bells, and landed in a pile at the Klauses' feet.

"Ouch," Mum said.

"My back!" Dad groaned.

"Moooore Christmas!" Ivy squealed.

The elf was the first to scramble up. He patted himself down and darted to Mr Klaus's side like a soldier standing to attention.

"Presenting . . ." he said in a ~~monsterous~~ monotonous tone, "the Carrolls."

The way he said 'Carrolls' made it sound like we were the most boring people on the planet.

"Actually," I said, thrusting my hand inside pocket number fifteen of my Hollyhood and throwing some snowflake confetti in the air. "We're the *Christmas* Carrolls!"

Before the snowflakes had fully settled on the ground,

Mrs Klaus clicked her fingers and the tall elf ran forward with a dustpan and brush (which he had somehow pulled out of thin air like a real, magical elf) and swept them all away. Then he took his place beside Mr Klaus again and stared into the distance as if we were completely invisible.

"And here's me thinking you'd be expert ice-skaters!" Mr Klaus chuckled, not bothering to help Dad up. "Don't worry, Big C. Maybe you can get a lesson or two from Ivan Yunu."

"Ivan Yunu?" Dad mumbled, untangling his apron strings from the bells on Mum's dress.

"The world's number one figure skater." Mr Klaus's smile was almost as big as Dad's. I actually found it quite unnervitating (a mixture of unnerving and irritating). "You must've heard of him?"

"Yes, yes, of course," Dad said, standing up and holding his aching back. "I've got a signed poster of him in my workshop."

"He just so happens to be one of our closest friends," Mrs Klaus added, her bright red lips drawing into a smile. "We've all trained with him, haven't we, kids? And he sent us diamond-white ice skates for Christmas last year."

The Klaus children nodded and smiled sweetly.

Diamond-white ice skates? Best friends with a professional ice-skater?

"Here," Mr Klaus said, handing Dad a silver envelope with a swirly K stamped across it. "Merry Christmas, Carroll family."

Dad took the envelope, wide-eyed. "But . . . how did you know we were coming?"

"We're always prepared for spreading cheer," Mr Klaus said smugly. "Aren't you?"

Dad's smile wavered. "Yes, well, er –"

"Of course," Mum spluttered. "But –"

"Here," I said, handing Mr Klaus a card that I'd found at the bottom of my Backpack of Cheer. "Merry Christmas, Klaus family."

Mr Klaus stared at the crumpled envelope, which was covered in stickers and glitter and a bit of Reggie's drool. I had been keeping it in my bag for the kind lady at the supermarket who collects money for charity, but I guessed I could always make her another one.

"Very good," Mr Klaus said. He smiled, but not in a cheery, beaming way this time. Then he turned to his wife. "Here you go, my angel. You can open it."

He passed the card to Mrs Klaus, who – without even looking at it – handed it straight to her son, who handed it to his sister, who pulled a face like she'd just eaten a rotten mince pie and . . .

dropped it

on

the

floor.

THE INTRODUCTIONS

11

I hated to admit it, but even I could feel my cheer-o-meter rating plummet. I was miles from home, the strap on my Backpack of Cheer had broken from the fall, and I was talking to strangers who wouldn't even read my Christmas card.

Mr Klaus brushed his hand through his thick head of hair, scratched his pointy chin, and ran his tongue across his blindingly white teeth. Mrs Klaus stood a whole thirty centimetres taller than her husband, with her hand on her hip and sucked-in cheeks so rosy I wondered if they'd been painted on. She played with her plaited hair, which was shaped to look like a giant snowflake on top of her head, and her crystal-blue eyes shone like the fairy lights on the house behind her.

I caught Mum staring at Mrs Klaus's hair as she tried to dislodge a bell or two from her own matted mess. Mum wasn't really the jealous type, but I could see a flicker of admiration in her eyes. If I was being completely honest, I felt the same way about the Klaus children. They were like miniature versions of their parents – all high cheekbones and long necks, sparkling eyes and confident smiles, perfectly styled hair and fur-lined Santa-style boots, and not a speck of dust or dirt on them.

Feeling embarrassed, I kicked my broken Backpack of Cheer behind me and tried to pick some paint splatters off my school uniform.

"I think some introductions are in order, don't you?" Mum said once she had wrestled the last jingling bell out of her bird's nest hair.

She'd put on a posh la-di-da voice that I'd never heard before. I tried so hard not to laugh out loud that

I very nearly wet myself. Even Dad couldn't hide his sniggering behind his enormous hands.

"Well then, I'm Nick," Dad said. "As in Nicholas. As in 'Old Saint Nicholas'. As in Father Christmas himself. Not that I'm saying *I'm* Father Christmas, of course, but, you know. We have similar names."

Mr and Mrs Klaus nodded, expressionless.

"And this is my wife, Snow," Dad continued.

Mum beamed, standing a little taller. "I wanted a name that reminded me of my favourite time of year," she said. "Do you like it?"

Mrs Klaus clasped her hands together. "Of course," she said. "It's very *cute*."

Cute? CUTE? I had always loved Mum's name. It impressed everyone we met, it was a great conversation starter, and it reminded us that Mum could take Christmas wherever she went. Anger grew in my belly like a lump of coal that had been set on fire. What was this woman's name, then? Something boring like 'Bob' or 'Bill' or 'Cardboard Box'? Actually, I quite liked the sound of someone being called Cardboard Box. Whatever her name was, I bet she wouldn't have known a good name if it hit her on the nose.

"My name is Santa," Mrs Klaus said.

Oh.

She let out a tittering laugh that sounded like a tinkleless bell. The fire in my belly got hotter.

"My full name is Santalaina," she continued. "But everyone calls me Laina. I don't think it's fair that I rub a name as wonderful as Santa in their face all the time, you know? I don't want people thinking I'm better than them just because I share the name of the greatest person on Earth."

"That's very, er, considerate of you," Mum said. "It's no wonder you made the final of the Most Festive Family competition."

~~Santa's~~ *Laina's* smile widened. "And this is my husband, Khris."

"Khris Kringle Klaus," Mr Klaus said, thrusting his giant chin in the air and licking his teeth. "No need to applaud. No need to applaud."

Laina gazed at her husband proudly. "And these are our perfect children, Poinsettia and Toboggan," she said, catching their eye and nodding as if giving them permission to move. Poinsettia spun around to reveal a giant red flower in her hair.

"Oh!" Mum gasped. "Poinsettia! Like the flower?"

"The *Christmas* flower," Poinsettia said, not bothering to smile back. "It's my trademark. I wear a poinsettia wherever I go."

"That's a bit like Holly's Hollyhood!" Mum said, pushing me so close to Poinsettia, I was basically looking up her nostrils. "She made it so she can take gifts with her wherever she goes. It's like a wearable advent calendar. See? You have your poinsettia flowers because your name is Poinsettia and Holly has her Hollyhood because –"

"This is my brother," Poinsettia said, clearly finished with the conversation. "His name is Toboggan. Like the wooden sleds people use to slide down hills."

Toboggan's cheeks turned red. "Toby is fine," he muttered.

Poinsettia grinned and then returned to gazing into the distance like a statue made of ice.

What was it with these people? Mum would say they were being 'less than cheerful'. Dad would call it 'passive aggressive'. I was just going to call it as I saw it. *Cold*. Colder than a yeti sleeping in the snow. Colder than an igloo trapped in a blizzard. Colder than Father Christmas without his –

"You must see Klausland before you go!" Mrs Klaus

clapped, pulling me out of my trance.

I glared at her. Cheers, lady. It wasn't like I was on a roll or anything.

"Klausland?" Mum said, her ears pricking up.

"What's that?" Dad asked.

"And where exactly do we have to go?" I added.

"Oh, not far," Laina said, clicking her fingers at the elf butler (who I might as well call the Elfler) to lead the way. "Just around the corner beyond those trees."

"Klausland is like Lapland but better," Poinsettia said, suddenly coming back to life. "It's what's going to win us the Most Festive Family competition."

"Now, now, Setti," Khris said, nodding his head as if to say she had a point. "A little healthy competition never hurt anyone."

Leaving my broken Backpack of Cheer behind us, Mum, Dad and I followed the Klauses and their Elfler around the corner of the house and through a line of perfectly symmetrical fir trees.

"Oh," I heard Mum gasp a few paces in front of me.

Oh what?

Oh no? Oh my? Oh dear?

My heart pounding, I burst through the trees ahead.

It took a moment for my eyes to adjust to the glare.

"Oh!"

KLAUSLAND

12

I t looked like ~~Santa's house village~~ ALL OF
LAPLAND had fallen into the Klauses' back
garden – if you could call it a garden.

The house sat at the very foot of a snowy mountain,
which was ten times taller than the surrounding trees. There
were rows and rows of sleds at the bottom and a ski lift to
transport people to the top. Giant, light-up letters stretched
across the middle to spell out the word KLAUSLAND. As
if introducing itself, an array of fireworks shot into the
sky as festive music played in the background.

I didn't know where to look first.

There was a café near the entrance to the ski lift

that was covered in multicoloured lights and a sign that read: *Klaus Café: Award-Winning Festive Food and Christmas Cocoa.* People dressed in elf costumes ran forward with trays of hot chocolate and individually wrapped mince pies.

Everything (and I mean EVERYTHING) had a fancy, swirly K on it. It was on the café workers' uniform, the front of the menus, the tablecloths draped over small, round tables, the hot chocolate mugs, the trays the elves were holding, the tiny boxes the mince pies were wrapped in, and even the pastry on top of the mince pies themselves.

"Well," Mrs Klaus said, shooing the café elves away. "Would you like to see the rest?"

Mum nodded. Dad gulped. Ivy squealed. I downed my hot chocolate so fast it scalded my throat.

"This is the Village Quarter of Klausland," Mrs Klaus said, swishing her fur-lined cape behind her. "We've got our award-winning café, a shop for borrowing ski suits and furs, stalls that sell stockings and wreaths, and a library that houses all the Christmas books from around the world."

Mum and Dad said "*WOW!*" simontaneously. I mean, symboltaneously. Singletaneously? SIM-UL-TAN-EE-OOS-LEE. Smashed it!

"Then over here we have the Ice Quarter," Mrs Klaus continued, guiding us through rows of shops and stalls that sold every kind of Christmas teapot you could imagine. "We have a year-round ice bar, igloos for Setti and Toby to have sleepovers in, and ice sculptures flown all the way from Alaska. You probably saw them in last year's *Best Homes* magazine?"

Dad smiled politely while Mum said, "Yes, yes, bravo," in the ridiculous posh voice she'd stumbled into.

"The Ice Quarter is centred around the Ice Lake," Mr Klaus explained, leading us around a lake that was easily four times the size of the one at the front of their house. "We've got ice bridges, ice caves and even an ice stage. That's where you'll find the dancing penguins."

"Dancing WHAT?" Dad cried.

Mrs Klaus did her silly tinkleless giggle. "Dancing penguins," she repeated as if we were stupid. "They've been specially trained for our entertainment and delight. Would you like to see their latest choreography?"

Red and green lights shot on to the lake as an elf hiding inside an ice hut saluted Mrs Klaus and played with some levers on his control pad.

"Tell you what," Mr Klaus said, already walking off with his giant chin leading the way. "Why don't the adults come with us? We can show you the house while the kids mess around with the silly ice dances."

"If you're sure?" Dad said, following Mr Klaus towards a clearing filled with snowmobiles. "I do fancy seeing your kitchen set-up. How many ovens do you have? Do you have a secret hot chocolate recipe? How many hours does it take you to cook the perfect turkey?"

What in all of Toyland was going on? How was Dad suddenly so obsessed with this family? And why was he taking Christmas advice from someone else? Had all the ice gone to his head?

"Come along, Snow," Mrs Klaus chirped.

It was more of a demand than a question and I did NOT appreciate someone telling my mum what to do.

Mum, on the other hand, had transformed into

someone I barely recognised.

"Spit spot, why not!" she said, the bells in her hair clunking together.

As Mum and Dad ran off after the Klauses in a state of absolute ~~awe~~ stupidity, I turned my attention to Setti and Toby. They seemed nice enough, but part of me yearned to be with Archer, Alice and Liena. Even though I was standing in a Christmas wonderland explosion, making masks for the Halloween Haunt somehow felt a billion times more festive.

"So I guess I'll hang here with you two," I said, shooting Setti and Toby my best 'let's be friends' smile. "What Christmas cheer shall we spread?"

THE NUISANCE

13

Setti and Toby ran towards the bridge that stretched across the middle of the ice lake. When they reached the bottom, they slipped their snow boots into some spiky slipper things and didn't even wait for me.

"Where's the Nuisance? Where's the Nuisance?" they chanted.

I slip-slid on to the ice bridge after them, realising a few seconds too late that I should probably have put some of those spiky slipper things on, too.

The elf inside the ice hut turned the volume up on the speakers. Before I knew what was happening, a barrage of white and black penguins wearing tiny bow ties flooded out of the ice cave and on to the lake. They shot in all directions, some following each other in zigzag lines and others spinning in unison like ballerinas in a music box. It was easily the most breathtaking yet bizarre thing I'd seen in my life.

"WHERE'S. THE. NUISANCE? WHERE'S. THE. NUISANCE?" Setti and Toby chanted loudly, slamming their fists on the icy bridge railing.

"What's the nuisance?" I said, finally catching up with them.

That was when I saw her. A baby penguin with a broken wing, one webbed foot bigger than the other and a tuft of feathers poking out of the top of her head stumbled on to the ice. She struggled to remain upright and her oversized flipper made her spin in circles, get instantizzy (instantly dizzy) and knock into the other penguins like a bowling ball hurtling towards a row of skittles.

"Sneezing Santa!" I cried. "Is she OK? Does she need our help?"

"HA HA HA HA!" Setti and Toby screeched, pointing at the poor penguin as she fell on to her back and struggled to get up.

"That foot of hers is so big, she should be a clown," Setti said, laughing louder.

"No," Toby replied, doubling over in hysterics. "Her foot is so big, it should have its own postcode!"

"Her foot is so big, she could trample a . . . a . . . a reindeer!" Setti howled with tears rolling down her cheeks.

"Her foot is so big, she can't even stand up straight!"

"Aren't you going to help her?" I said, my heart suddenly feeling heavier than Santa's sack.

Setti and Toby slowly turned to look at me.

"Where's the fun in that?" Setti scowled.

"Yeah. Where's the fun in that?" sneered Toby.

My mind raced, thinking of all the different ways I could spread cheer to the poor penguin. "How about tying some tinsel around our waists and abseiling off the bridge to save her?" I said. "Or we could make a rope from fairy lights and lasso her from the side? Or even make a little wooden sleigh and slide it on to the ice like we're on a secret rescue mission?"

Setti and Toby looked at me as though I'd just farted the alphabet.

"And why would we waste our time doing that?" Toby said.

"Waste our time?" I said, watching the baby penguin tremble nervously as the others skated around her. "She needs our help. We need to spread some cheer. We need to do the Christmassy thing."

"So you think you're more Christmassy than us?" Setti said, folding her arms across her chest. "You think you know it all? You think you're going to win the Most Festive Family competition, is that what you're saying?"

"No," I said, flapping my arms like the penguins

on the ice. "I just want to help her. She's struggling."

"She's *learning*," Toby corrected. "Learning to be perfect."

"Because anything less than perfect isn't worth having," Setti and Toby said together.

"Of course, families like *the Carrolls* have to settle for less than perfect," Setti said, shrugging her shoulders. "But you do your best, I suppose."

Families like the Carrolls? What did she mean? I knew we were a bit ~~electric~~ eccentric and not everyone celebrated Christmas all year round, but the Klauses loved Christmas just as much as us (although I hated to admit it). How were we any different?

"Mother and Father give us anything we want," Toby said, sticking his nose in the air. "They can afford the best of the best of the best, so why have anything less?"

"But Christmas isn't about affording the best. It's –"

"I'm bored," Setti said, grabbing the sides of her cloak and sliding back down the bridge on her bum. "Come on, Toby."

As the music died down and the penguins skated back into their ice cave, the elf came out of his hut and helped the injured penguin on to her feet. Her little head darted from left to right like she didn't know where to look and her whole body was shivering.

"Are you coming or not?" Toby said, sliding down the bridge after Setti. "You won't like it when the lights go out. It's dark and no one brings you hot chocolate or presents unless they know where you are."

I checked that ~~the Nuisance~~ the baby penguin was safe. She looked lost, confused, and in serious need of a yeti hug. It was exactly how I felt when I joined Lockerton Primary School, and I wanted to help her so much my heart ached.

There wasn't time for hesitation, though. Setti and Toby had stormed ahead and were almost out of sight. I ran after them, twisting my head to check that the penguin was OK. And true to Toby's word, as soon as we disappeared into the next section of Klausland, the lights in the Ice Village went out.

"Which quarter are we going into next?" I said, half expecting to find Santa and his elves having a party in the middle of Klausland.

"The best one," Setti said, not bothering to look back. "The Toy Quarter."

THE TOY QUARTER

14

I felt like I'd fallen into a dream. How else could you explain the three-metre teddy bears that blinked and waved and wished you a 'Merry Christmas' as you walked past? Or the life-size action figures and dolls, giant robots and towering music boxes that had real-life ballerinas twirling inside? There was even a golden steam train that clickety-clacked around the Toy Quarter with multicoloured bubbles puffing out of its chimney.

"What's that smell?" I said, stumbling after Setti and Toby as they jumped across a piano path and hopscotched their way through a Lego brick maze.

"Sweets," Toby said, looking at me with one impressively high, raised eyebrow. "Duh."

We exited the Lego maze and found ourselves face to face with hundreds of lollipops, candy canes and gummy bears. They were at least three times as tall as me, and they led to the Klauses' Toy Workshop, which was hidden inside the mountain beside the house.

"This is *all* yours?" I said, pinching myself in case Reggie had headbutted me in the bath and I had passed out on the floor, dreaming every second of this weird and wonderful place.

"Yep," Setti said. "Unless a celebrity comes to visit.

Or a news reporter. Then Mother and Father make us share it."

"You mean you don't invite anyone over?" I said, wondering why in jingling bells anyone would need ALL of this for themselves. "What about children who are less fortunate? Or those who don't get a real Christmas? What about raising money for a charity by opening it up like a theme park for the day?"

"Raising money?" Toby tutted.

"*Charity?*" Setti groaned. "You think *we* are a charity?"

"If we give all of this away, then we won't have anything for ourselves," Toby said. "You Carrolls aren't very bright, are you?"

"Toby!" Setti scolded, whacking him on the shoulder. "It's not polite to point out people's flaws."

I felt my shoulders relax.

"Especially when they're as deluded as this lot," Setti concluded.

Whatever 'dee-loo-did' meant, it wasn't good. Setti and Toby smirked at each other and waited for my reaction.

Spread cheer, I told myself, trying to find something to compliment Setti and Toby on. *Spread cheer, not fear.*

"I, er, I like your slide," I said, pointing at a curved piece of metal that twisted around the mountain and ended near the back of the Klauses' oversized house.

"Slide?" Setti snapped, her lip curling towards her nose. "Did you just call our prize-winning toboggan a *slide*?"

"But it looks like a slide," I said, confused.

"Our great, great, great, great, great grandfather

invented the toboggan," Setti sharply informed me. "That's who Toby is named after. His full name is Toboggan Tinsel Tidings Klaus. Impressive, isn't it?"

My eyes narrowed. And what was *her* name? Poinsettia Pinecone Poo-face Klaus?

"*Very* impressive," I said, reminding myself to think cheerful thoughts.

"HO, HO, HO!" Dad's laugh rang through the sugar-coated trees. "This is merrynifiscent!"

A few seconds later, Mr and Mrs Klaus skidded their snowmobiles to a stop and Mum and Dad hopped off. They were practically giddy with . . . what was that? Cheer? Excitement? Travel sickness?

"We wish we didn't have to depart," Mum said, pulling me in for a big bear hug. "We've had a spiffing time, but it's a school night and darling Holly has homework and such."

Homework and such? Spiffing? Depart? What was Mum turning into?

"Snow's right," Dad said, his eye twitching slightly.

"And clearly we've got A LOT to do before the editor from *The Christmas Chronicle* arrives in eleven days."

The Klauses smiled.

"Well then," Mr Klaus said, showing us back through the Ice Quarter, the Village Quarter, through the symmetrical fir trees and out into their . . . driveway? Courtyard? Theme-park entrance? "We'd have you stay for a glass of eggnog if we could. It's made on site by our very own eggnog chef. He's perfected the best eggnog recipe in the world. Very expensive stuff. But I'm sure your tastebuds aren't accustomed to such . . . *rich* . . . aromas."

"Not to worry," Dad said. "We have our own eggnog recipe. Top secret. Top, top secret. Old family recipe. Passed down for generations. Never tasted anything like it."

Mr Klaus laughed. "Cheery-ho, then."

Dad's eyebrow twitch intensified. Oh no. Why hadn't he thought of that? 'Cheery' mixed with 'ho-ho-ho'? CHEERY-HO? He looked like he'd just smelled one of Reggie's nuclear farts.

"We really must be going now," Dad said, swiping my Backpack of Cheer off the ground and swinging the broken strap over his shoulder. "Come on, Carrolls."

Mum buckled Ivy into her car seat and did a weird curtsey. "It's been frightfully cheering to meet you," she said as the Klauses lined up outside their door with the Elfler beside them. "We've had a golly jolly good time."

Dad dragged her into the car and turned the engine on.

"Smile and wave," he muttered, thrusting his hand out the window. "Just smile and wave and let's get out of here."

The Klauses stood like statues as we drove past the snow fountains, through the twinkling tunnel of trees and towards the main gates into Candy Cane Lane. As soon as we got past the security elf-ficer, Dad put his foot down. Sweat dripped down his brow as his shoulders tensed and his knuckles tightly gripped the steering wheel.

"WHAT JUST HAPPENED?" he bellowed.

"We can't compete with the Klauses!" Mum cried.

"They've got a butler."

"They've got a ski mountain."

"They have their own toy workshop."

"They have dancing penguins."

"They . . . they. . ."

Mum and Dad looked at each other.

"They have *everything*."

THE
BROKEN
BACKPACK
OF CHEER

15

I jolted awake. Dad was clattering extra loudly in the kitchen, Mum was singing her morning carols in the garden, and Ivy was wailing 'Christmas, Christmas, Christmaaaas!' to let everyone know that she was awake.

Blearily, I pushed my snowflake curtains to one side and peered down the street.

Pumpkins in the neighbours' gardens? Check.

Orangey-red leaves falling from the trees? Check.

Not a single ski mountain or mirrored driveway in sight? Check.

I chuckled to myself. Of course! It *had* all been a dream. How could I have been so –

Then I saw it.

My Backpack of Cheer, the broken strap, Santa's squished face, and a . . . a . . . a BABY PENGUIN?

I jumped back. What in roasted chestnuts was an *actual penguin* doing in my bedroom?

The penguin slid under my bed and nestled inside a pile of jumpers I'd been knitting for Santa's reindeer. She was almost entirely hidden except for one large webbed foot poking out at the bottom.

"Oh," I said, crouching down to get a better look. "It's *you*."

The penguin gazed back at me, her broken flipper hanging limply beside her body.

"How did you get here?" I asked.

The penguin's eyes flitted to my Backpack of Cheer. She peeped softly. It was almost like she was apologising.

"Oh," I said again, noticing the stretched seams and broken strap on my backpack. "I see. So you hid in my backpack to escape?"

The penguin shook nervously.

"It's OK," I whispered, trying to find my calm voice (although, to be honest, I don't think I've got one). "I'm not angry. Everyone's welcome here."

The penguin looked at me, unsure.

"I'm Holly," I said, gently extending my arm. "And you're the Nu–"

The penguin looked away.

"What I mean, is, er . . ." My brain whirred. Nuisance. Nu. New. Yes, NEW! "What I mean is, you're my *newest* friend," I said.

Slowly, *very* slowly, the penguin edged out from under the bed. With a little help from me, she finally stood upright, her tiny tuft of feathers poking out of her head like a fountain of fluff.

"Shall we find you a new name?" I said, stroking her soft, slippery feathers. "A new name for a new friend?"

The penguin nuzzled into me and my heart turned gooey like the warm butter we used to make gingerbread houses. She was so calm. So quiet. So the complete opposite to me!

"What about Snowball?" I said.

The penguin backed away a little.

"Frostbite?"

The penguin shook her head.

"Iglooana?"

The penguin covered her eyes with her unbroken flipper.

I laughed. "Maybe not. Hmmm, what about . . . Nuisa– Nu-Si– Nu-Su– SUE!"

The penguin flapped her good flipper and stamped her oversized foot in excitement.

I beamed. "It's tinselriffic to meet you, Sue."

I held my arm out again. Sue waddled towards me and gave me a high five.

"WOW!" I laughed, wishing I had the Christmacam nearby. "Who taught you how to do that? You're a very special penguin."

Sue lowered her head. She obviously wasn't used to getting ~~condiments~~ compliments.

"Well then," I said, shoving on my school uniform

and wrapping my Hollyhood so fast around my neck
I nearly strangled myself. "I guess we should tell Mum
and Dad that we've got a new member of the family.
And such a beautiful one!"

Sue flapped her good flipper and ran to hide behind
the curtain.

"It's OK," I said. "We're the Carrolls, remember?
We spread cheer, not fear?"

Slowly, a tiny clump of feathers and one beady eye
poked out from behind the curtain.

"Mum and Dad are going to love you," I said. "You wait and see! Let me look at that broken flipper first, and then I'll introduce you."

Sue peeped three times, which I can only assume meant 'Thank you, Holly', 'Merry Christmas, Holly' or 'I'm hungry, Holly.' She was going to fit in perfectly!

THE SUE-TUATION

16

"NO!" Mum cried, making Sue jump so high that she landed on her back and needed help to get up again. "Sue belongs to the Klauses, Holly! You can't just take someone else's things. That's stealing! It's theft. It's KIDNAPPING!"

"Actually, it's penguin-napping," I said.

"Holly Carroll, I thought we taught you better than that," Dad said, sticking his 'Eggnog Recipe Attempt 102' on the wall with gloopy, sugary fingers. "What would you do if someone strode in and took Reggie?"

"But I didn't take her!" I argued. "She escaped. She wanted to get out. We're saving her."

"Saving her from the wonderful ice palace with its daily dance routines?" Mum said, shaking her head in that really annoying *I'm so disappointed in you, Holly Carroll* kind of way. "The Klauses gave Sue everything she could ever dream of at Klausland. Why would she want to escape?"

I looked at Sue sadly. Why didn't Mum and Dad get it? Had the Klauses blinded them with their sparkly home and enormous theme-park garden? Were they letting all the diamonds and expensive eggnog recipes cloud their fudgement?

I huffed. "Christmas doesn't shine out of their back—"

"Garden!" Dad shouted, waving his wooden spoon in the air. "We *must* figure out what we can do with the back garden, Snow. Did you see how they've separated theirs into four sections? Maybe we can divide ours into EIGHT? Maybe the neighbours will let us take down the fences and use their land? Maybe we could make a toboggan run that's twice as long as the Klauses' and have it twirling around the neighbours' chimneys?"

"Winterful!" Mum said, momentarily forgetting about me and Sue to scribble a new Christmas cracker design on the corner of Dad's recipe book. "The Klauses have penguins and ice rinks. Maybe we can have polar bears and parties? Wouldn't that be frostastic? We could get a disco ball and everything."

"That all sounds great," I said, watching Sue skid under the kitchen table. "But what am I meant to do about this situation? I mean . . . *sue*-tuation?" (You could see that one coming, couldn't you?)

"You'll just have to take her back to the Klauses," Mum said. "And hope that they haven't realised she's missing. If they have, they might not be our friends any more."

I tutted. "You think the Klauses are your friends?"

"You'd better go as soon as school is finished, Holly," Dad said. "We can't risk them telling the editor of *The Christmas Chronicle*! What would he think of us?"

"But Daaaaad," I groaned. "Can't I stay home with Sue? Just for today?"

"Out of the question," Dad said sternly (er, when was Dad ever stern?). "We've got electricians coming to install more fairy lights. I need to clean all the carpets ready for a fresh layer of indoor snow. And the hedges outside are being trimmed to look like Santa's elves."

"And that's just this morning!" Mum added, chucking cartons of milk and bags of sugar across the kitchen. Dad caught the milk mid-air and the sugar inside his Santa hat. "Someone's coming to sweep the chimney, I want to make a walk-through Snow Carroll showcase with all of the Christmas aprons I've made over the last thirty years, and I want to write a new Christmas song that we can record and play for the editor of *The Christmas Chronicle*."

"HEE-HAW!" Reggie bawled, stampeding through the back door and running in circles around the kitchen table. "HEEEE-HAAAW!"

"Not now, Reggie!" Dad cried, falling over Reggie and dropping an entire carton of milk. "This isn't the time for flying practice."

Reggie tried to stop, but he misjudged the length of the kitchen and crashed into the coat cupboard instead. He emerged a few seconds later with a bobble hat on the end of his nose, a snowman apron across his back, and a sparkly glove on the end of his tail. It would actually have been a good look if Mum hadn't rushed over, swiped everything off and shoved him back into the garden.

"I'm sorry, Reginald," she said. "There's no time for fun and games today. I know you like to have your breakfast with us, but you'll have to eat it outside. We've got too many other things to worry about this morning."

Reggie's ears drooped.

"But Reggie always has breakfast with us!" I said, wondering if I could hide a diva donkey, a nervous penguin and myself inside the coat cupboard until Mum and Dad calmed down a bit. "And pleeease can Sue stay?"

"The penguin goes back tonight," Mum said, losing all cheer and jolliness from her voice. "Your father and I have a lot to deal with right now, Holly. Did you *see* the Klauses' house last night?"

"Yes."

"Then you'll know that we need all hands on deck-orations. Just go to school, return the penguin and then help us make a stocking for the editor, OK?"

"But I was going to see my friends tonight," I groaned. "We were going to do our homework. And make sweets for trick-or-treaters. And I was going to show Alice and Liena our special way of wrapping candy. And it was going to be amazing and not at all scary. Pur-leeease can I go?"

"There will be plenty of time to play with your friends once this Christmas competition is over," Dad said. It was obvious he was only half-listening. He didn't even blink when I said I wanted to do something Halloweeny. "Why don't you keep Sue in your room today? That way, you can go to school and she won't get under our feet."

Sue looked at her oversized foot and let out a quiet, drawn-out peep. I sighed.

"Magical mistletoe!" Dad cried, checking the time and tearing off his Christmas pudding apron. "I need to get you to school, Hols. Come on, come on! Snow much to do. Snow little time."

Sue looked at me with ~~puppy-dog~~ baby-penguin eyes. They were small and black and round and helpless, and in an instant, I knew there was only one thing to do.

Quietly, I took her good flipper and guided her into the hallway. Surrounded by Christmas trees, giant ice sculptures and nutcracker wallpaper, I emptied the pens and pencils from my Backpack of Cheer and stuffed them inside my tinsel-covered October stocking instead.

"Sue?" I said, holding the empty bag open. "Have you ever been to school?"

PENGUINS DON'T LIVE IN BACKPACKS

17

"There is no way you have a penguin in your backpack, Holly," Archer said, folding his arms across his chest as I pulled him around the back of the Year Five block. "Penguins don't live in backpacks, or magically turn up out of thin air."

I pulled open my Backpack of Cheer.

Sue popped her head out.

Archer let out a sound like he'd seen a ghost with an exploding head.

"Holly!" he hissed, jumping back. "It's . . . it's . . ."

"A penguin," I said, trying to keep my voice down so I didn't startle her. "I did tell you."

"But what on earth is it doing at school?" Archer gasped.

It took me ages to fill Archer in. I explained what had happened at the Klauses' house, how Sue had hidden in the Backpack of Cheer, and how Mum and Dad were acting strangely now that they were spending every waking second trying to out-Christmas the Klauses.

"And now they're expecting me to take her back. This afternoon. Straight after school. Mum's going to drive me so Dad can practise making *risengynsgrøt* and then –"

"Rise-and-shine-what?"

"*Risengynsgrøt*," I said, waving my hand in the air like it was the least of our concerns. "It's a hot rice pudding they serve in Norway at Christmas. Dad wants to cook something from every country in the world that celebrates Christmas. And when I get back from returning Sue, he wants me to make a Christmas drink to rival the Klauses' hot chocolate."

"I guess that means you can't come to mine to make Halloween sweets?" Archer said, unable to take his eyes off the baby penguin.

My heart dropped. How could I explain that Dad didn't even listen to me when I mentioned it earlier? How could I say that I was (almost) excited by the idea of making Halloween sweets, but there was no way my parents would let me do anything un-Christmassy right now? How could I say yes to Archer and yes to my parents and not let anyone down?

"I can't, Archie," I said, stroking Sue's slippery flipper. "This Christmas competition is too important."

Archer did a head-shake-nod thing, like he only half understood. Then he went back to staring at Sue.

"You're really going to keep her in your bag all day?" he said, crouching down but keeping his distance. "What if someone sees her?"

I looked around the playground. I'd already spotted two zombie masks, a witch's cloak, a pumpkin hat and a skeleton flag.

"Everyone's thinking about Halloween," I said, still trying to get used to the idea of spending the next couple of weeks surrounded by werewolves and vampires and aliens from outer space. "They won't be paying any attention to the crazy Christmas girl."

"They will if they know you've brought an actual penguin into school!"

I placed the Backpack of Cheer on my shoulder. Sue gave a little peep and then settled on top of the knitted stockings I'd stuffed at the bottom of the bag.

"Hey, Holly! Archer!" Alice shouted, sliding towards us on her skateboard. "Are you guys doing anything this weekend? Liena and I were going to use the leftover mask fabric to make some decorations for the Halloween Haunt. Wanna help?"

"Decorations?" I said, eyeing up her skateboard and thinking how much it looked like a miniature sleigh.

"Like bunting and stockings and fairy lights?"

"Sort of," she said with a smile. "But with cobwebs and red food colouring and squishy eyeballs, too."

"If I come, could I also have a go on your skateboard?" I asked.

Alice stamped her foot on one end of the board and sent it flying into the air. "Any time," she said, catching it with one hand and holding it out towards me. "Does that mean you're coming?"

"I'll be there!" Archer said. "And I'll bring my skateboard, too."

I hesitated before answering. "I'd really like to," I said quietly. "Can I let you know?"

Alice nodded. "I've invited some other people from Year Five," she said, hopping back on to her skateboard and zooming away. "Please try to come, Holly! I know we're not doing anything Christmassy but we're doing something together and that's kind of the same thing."

Alice's words hit me like that time I accidentally ran into a three-metre nutcracker. It was like my heart had jolted and my brain had flipped and my eyes could suddenly see things more clearly.

Christmas was about being together. It was about making memories. It was about spreading cheer any way you can and that included making decorations for a school party. Surely Mum and Dad would understand that? Surely they'd let me go if I explained? Surely I could find a way to enjoy *some* parts of Halloween?

I spent the whole morning wondering if Halloween was as awful as Mum and Dad had made it out to be, but then something happened that was so terrifying, so shocking, so ghastly, so hideous, I thought my heart might stop.

"You've LOST Sue?" Archer shouted.

"Shhhh!" I hissed, dragging Archer into the playground as soon as the bell rang for lunch. "She was there at break time. She was there during maths when she kept pecking my leg. And she was there ten minutes ago when I dropped my Hollyhood on the floor and snuck her some tinned anchovies from Dad's Christmas Eve cupboard."

"Anchovies?" Archer said, pulling a face like I'd just presented him with reindeer poo. "On Christmas Eve?"

"Yes!" I said, peering under benches and behind rubbish bins. "Some people in Piedmont – that's in Italy – spread cheer by making *bagna cauda* out of anchovies and eating it on Christmas Eve. Then there's people in Tuscany who make *pappa al pomodoro* out of anchovies and that's a big part of their meal on Christmas Eve. And then there's the pastalicious *ammuddicata*, which is eaten on Christmas Eve in Sicily and it's made from breadcrumbs aaaand . . ."

Archer looked at me as though he was about to ask a million more anchovy questions.

"Forget anchovies!" I yelled, flapping my arms impatiently. "We need to find Sue!"

As we ~~scowled~~ scoured the school, we couldn't see a tiny white and black penguin anywhere. Clown masks?

Yep. Broomsticks? A whole bunch. Fake plastic spiders? Everywhere. But penguins? NOPE.

"Holly?" Archer grumbled, checking the hall for the fourth time and even climbing on to the lost-property bin to peek into Mrs Spencer's office. "I'm hungry. And lunchtime is nearly over. What are we going to do?"

"We could tell the head teacher?" I said, climbing up beside Archer.

"That's possibly the worst idea you've ever had!" Archer said. "Dan got detention for bringing his PlayStation into school on his birthday. What do you think Mrs Spencer would do if she knew you'd brought in an actual penguin?"

"Well, we can't just —"

The back door to the school hall swung open and smacked against the wall.

"Shut the freezer door, Ellie! Someone left it open earlier," a man shouted, wheeling a cart down an alley that ran around the back of the hall. "And then lock up, will you?"

Archer and I looked at each other.

Freezers.

Cold.

Penguins!

"Are you thinking what I'm thinking?" I said, jumping off the lost-property bin and clip-clopping across the playground like a reindeer that had proudly nailed a difficult landing.

"Quickly!" Archer yelled, following my lead but missing out the fun clip-clop part. "Before the door shuts!"

ANCHOVY PIE

Archer sprinted ahead and shoved his foot in the frame to stop the door from slamming. Then, imagining I was Father Christmas slipping into a house on Christmas Eve, I ducked under his arm and tiptoed towards the kitchens.

"Excuse me, young man?" said a woman's voice. "You shouldn't be there."

Archer waved his hand at me to go, then turned to face whoever had arrived. "Hello!" he said a bit too enthusiastically. "Can I, er, ask you a question? About, er . . . FOOD? Yes, food."

"I really don't think –"

"Did you know some people eat anchovies on Christmas Eve?" Archer spluttered.

I crept down the corridor and into the kitchen as fast as I could. Everything was shiny. And silver. And cold. It reminded me of the Klauses' house and made me shiver.

"I'd like to make an anchovy pie!" I heard Archer yell somewhere behind me. "Yeah. An anchovy pie."

"An anchovy pie?" I could hear the distaste in the woman's voice.

"That's right!" Archer's voice was high-pitched and panicky. "On Christmas Eve. Like they do in Italy."

"It's a bit early to think about Christmas Eve, isn't it? We haven't even got to Halloween yet."

"It's never too early to spread cheer," Archer replied without hesitation.

I stopped in my tracks as a warm, fuzzy feeling filled my heart. If there was an official Best Friend Award, Archer should win it, hands down.

"So, yeah, anyway . . . could you, like, tell me how

you'd make an anchovy pie?"

There was silence for a moment. Then a scuttling of feet across the corridor and a giant thud of a cupboard door being shut.

"I guess I can spare five minutes. I'm sure I've got something in this recipe book . . ."

While Archer asked his first question ("What ingredients do I need?"), I crawled around on my hands and knees, trying to find Sue. At his next question ("How do you spell 'anchovy'?"), I bashed my head on a shelf of saucepans and thanked my lucky Santa suit that Archer's nervous, squealy voice had blocked out most of the noise. As he asked what sort of spoon they'd use to mix the pastry, I accidentally crawled head first into a stack of wobbling lunch trays. And just when it sounded like he was running out of questions, he asked the best one of all ("What's an anchovy?") – and I spotted a large, humming silver door.

The freezer! It looked like Ellie had closed it, like she'd been asked. I rushed forward, grabbed the handle, heaved the door open, and . . .

No Sue.

Weird. There was ice on the walls and everything. It was the perfect spot for a penguin. Where WAS she?

I closed the freezer door and searched every nook and cranny of the kitchen. She wasn't behind a bubbling pot of tomatoey-smelling liquid. She wasn't inside a human-size pack of frozen peas. And she wasn't underneath a huge crate of tea and biscuits that had a sign attached to them that said 'DO NOT TOUCH. MRS SPENCER'S SECRET STASH'.

Just when I thought I'd lost Sue forever, I heard a tiny peep that made my heart swell.

The noise came from a gap between the oven and the wall. When I looked closer, I could just see the tip of a webbed foot poking out.

"SUE!" I cried. "You scared me half to death! And if there's one thing I don't like, it's being scared!"

Sue eased herself out from beside the oven and nuzzled into my armpit. We stayed like that for a few moments, until the warmth from the oven and the tickle of Sue's feathers calmed my nerves.

When we finally let go, Sue began twirling around the kitchen, using her large, webbed foot to catapult herself into the air and her one good flipper to make shapes in the air like a ballerina.

"Sue!" I gasped, watching her spin around. "You're a tinselriffic dancer! I bet you could teach Prancer and Dancer a thing or two!"

Sue let out a little peep and bowed mid-twirl. I watched her in awe, wondering why she was so clumsy and awkward on the Klauses' ice rink when she was actually the most talented dancer I'd ever seen. She wasn't tripping over her giant foot. She wasn't making herself dizzy. And she wasn't bumping into anything or falling on to her back. In fact, Sue looked more at home in the warm Lockerton Primary School kitchens than in all of snowy, icy, freezing-cold Klausland.

"THAT'S IT!" I cried, trying to memorise her routine so I could join in later. "You prefer the warm, don't you?" I thought back to the jumpers she burrowed into under my bed and the snuggly stocking she slept on inside my Backpack of Cheer. Now, here she was, finding comfort in front of an oven! "That's why you can't dance in Klausland," I said. "That's why you wanted to escape. *You don't like the cold!*"

Before Sue could answer, Archer poked his head around the kitchen door. "We've got to go," he cried. "I've run out of questions and Ellie wants to lock up and . . . IS THAT SUE?"

Sue lifted her one good flipper to wave and danced dreamily around the room. She was the happiest I'd ever seen her.

"Isn't she snowtacular?" I said happily.

"Yes," Archer breathed. "But she's got to go back, Holly. You know that."

I stayed quiet for a moment, trapped in thought. "Will you help me put everything right, Arch?"

Archer nodded. "Of course. We'll just go the Klauses', sneak into the Ice Quarter and –"

"Convince them to set Sue free," I said in determination. "Yes."

"Wait," said Archer. "WHAT?"

THE PENGUIN PLAN

19

The end of the school day couldn't come quick enough. I had tried to hide Sue inside my Hollyhood, but the tuft of feathers on top of her head kept tickling my chin and after the third time of squealing out loud in the middle of a very serious science lesson, Miss Eversley told me to calm myself in the corridor and 'only come back when you're ready to act appropriately'.

It didn't make much sense, if I'm being totally honest. How else were you meant to act when you were being tickled? Turn red and get angry? Start snoring and fall asleep? Suddenly get overwhelmingly hungry and eat everything in sight?

I ended up hiding Sue inside my Backpack of Cheer and wearing it on my front like a mum carrying a baby in a sling. Every now and then I had to pretend to sneeze or cough when Sue started peeping for another anchovy. When it was almost home time, I pretended to fart to disguise a particularly loud peep, but the *peep PARP!* just made everyone laugh and Miss Eversley gave me a look as if to say, *Do that again and you'll have another time out in the corridor.*

I'm telling you, friends, being a school student was hard, but being a penguin mum was even harder.

On the way out of school, almost everyone wanted to wish me a Terrific Tuesday or ask what costume I was wearing to the Halloween Haunt. I should've been happy that they were including me. That they were excited to see what sort of outfit I could fashionise. But I had no idea how Mum and Dad would react, and even if I did sort of, a tiny bit (maybe a lot) want to go to the Halloween Haunt, all I could focus on in that moment was getting Sue home without anyone seeing her.

As Dad drove Archer and me home, I wondered whether I should write a letter to Father Christmas to find out exactly how he did it. I mean, the man flew around the world with eight reindeer, a huge golden sleigh and a never-ending sack of presents without ever getting caught, and I could barely get out of the school gates with a baby penguin hidden in my bag. If only he could send me a tiny bit of Christmas magic. It wouldn't need to be a lot. Just a sprinkle down the chimney. A secret spell written in a card. He could sneeze Christmas snot all over me if that would give me secret invisibility powers. I wouldn't mind.

"So, ho, ho," Dad said, wearing three Santa hats and blasting his Christmas car playlist extra loudly. "We've got a lot done today, Snowflake. Carroll Town is coming along nicely, but there's no time to stop if we want to compete with Klausland. Do you think you and Archer can hop on the bus to return that penguin? Then we need you back sharpish to help with our preparations for *The Christmas Chronicle*."

Sue poked her head out of my bag. I had to coax her back inside with another slimy anchovy before Dad spotted her.

"I was going to take you to the Klauses' myself," Dad continued, oblivious to the smell of fish and the nervous fart I'd just let out. "But I've got a meeting with Lockerton Council to arrange a Christmas parade on the day the editor wants to visit. Wouldn't that be something? A Christmas parade. On Sleigh Ride Avenue. In October!"

Ordinarily, Dad's Christmas cheer wouldn't faze me. His energy, enthusiasm and passion for Christmas was one of the reasons I loved him so much. But this energy was different. It came with a talking-really-fast voice, twitching brows and eyes that looked like they hadn't slept in a week. I wondered if now was the right time to mention the Halloween Haunt or making decorations at Alice's house.

Dad started muttering his to-do list under his breath.

No. Maybe not.

"Are we actually calling it Carroll Town?" I said, winding the window down so Sue could feel some wind through her feathers. "Isn't that copying?"

"It's nothing of the sort! The Klauses have Klaus LAND. We have Carroll TOWN. They're two very different things, Hols." Dad proceeded to tell us about the hot-chocolate fountains he wanted to install, the ski slope he wanted to build off the roof, and how he was going to become an official eggnog expert by the end of the week.

"That all sounds great," I said. "But can I talk to you about something else for a second?"

"Like what?" Dad said, smiling at me in the rear-view mirror. "Christmas pyjamas? Christmas plates? Ooh, what about that singing Santa shower head I mentioned the other day?"

"I actually had something else in mind," I said, staring out of the window. "I, er, I wondered if I could go to a party?"

"A party? I love a party! When is it?"

I gulped. "On the same day as the editor's visit."

Dad's shoulders dropped. "But it's our Christmas rehearsal, Snowflake. You can't miss that. It's our one chance. Our only opportunity. You'll have plenty more parties to go to."

I took a deep breath and scrunched my eyes. "But this one is the Halloween Haunt," I said quickly before I changed my mind. "All of my friends are going and

I don't want to miss it and I don't even think it'll be that scary."

Dad's foot momentarily slipped off the pedal.

"It's our *Christmas* rehearsal," he said firmly. "Less spreading fear, more spreading cheer, hey, Hols?"

GOLLY JOLLY HOLLY

20

I KNEW it. Mum and Dad were totally against Halloween. Dad's reaction proved it. Did that mean I could never ever do anything but knit Christmas stockings, bake festive cookies and shout about Santa from the rooftops? Could I not at least *try* something different?

"Right then," Dad said, so eager to get away from all the Halloween talk, he forgot to take his seat belt off. "Your mum has made you some snowiches for the journey . . ." – he wrestled with the seat belt like it was some tightly wound ribbon he was trying to tear off a present – ". . . and if you jump on the number 303 bus, that'll take you to the main bus terminal. Then switch over to bus number 489 and that'll take you to the road that leads to Candy Cane Lane. You can be there by five thirty if you're quick. Just drop the penguin off, tell the guard it was a big mistake and come straight back for dinner and carols and eggnog testing."

I grumpily grabbed the snowiches from Mum, which she'd stuffed inside red velvet stockings, and stomped down the street towards the bus stop with Archer. How could Dad shoot me down like that? How could he totally ignore my request to go to the Halloween Haunt and then go back to being his jolly, jovial self like it was snow big deal?

"So what do we do now?" Archer said, munching on an ice cake from his stocking. "How are you planning to convince the Klauses to set Sue free?"

"The plan has changed, Arch," I said, feeling the knots in my stomach tighten as the number 303 bus turned into the road. "It's time to do something *I* want to do for a change."

Archer stopped munching. "Oh? What's that?"

I found three empty seats at the back of the bus and put my Backpack of Cheer on the window seat. "It's time to set ALL of the penguins free."

Archer was normally really good at going along with whatever Christmassiness I came up with. But trespassing on the Klauses' property and smuggling a load of penguins out *may* have been a step too far.

"Holly," he said, looking up and down the deserted street as we approached the sign for Candy Cane Lane. "This is nuts. Like, seriously nuts. How are we meant to –"

"HELLO!" I beamed, stuffing a candy cane in my mouth so I could wave at the security elf-ficer with both hands. "D'YU LEMEMBER EE?"

The security elf-ficer poked his head out of his stripy hut and squinted at me.

"I'm at school with Setti and Toby Klaus," I said, taking the candy cane out of my mouth and jumping over the tinsel-covered barrier before he could stop me. Archer followed me and nervously hid his hands in his pockets. "I was here the other day with my mum and dad?"

The security elf-ficer's eyes drew closer together. "I don't –"

"Setti let me borrow one of her dancing penguins," I said, holding Sue above my head like that famous scene in *The Lion King*. "I promised her I'd return it today. And I don't want to be late. You know how the Klauses don't like to be kept waiting."

The security elf-ficer looked us up and down. His spiky moustache bristled. "You don't wear the same school uniforms as the Klaus children," he said.

"That's because they have their own *special* uniform," I said, my own eyes bulging at how impressively quickly I was coming up with these ~~lies untruths~~ stories. "The Klauses like to be different. They wouldn't ever let anyone wear the same old uniform as them."

"Holly," Archer hissed. "I really don't think this is going to –"

"You've got a point," the security elf-ficer said, slumping back down in his seat. "Just sign in here, grab a Klauspass, and follow the road around. If you get lost, call out the password three times and I'll come find you."

"What's the password?" Archer said, looking extra panicky.

"It's on the Klauspass," the elf-ficer said, handing us both a silver lanyard to wear like a necklace. "Along with the guest WiFi code, visiting hours, and what the Klauses would like for Christmas this year."

"Golly Jolly Holly," Archer said, reading the back of the Klauspass.

"Or 'Holly Jolly Golly' if there's a fire and you need to urgently turn the sprinklers on," the elf-ficer added. "Probably best not to get the two mixed up."

"I can't believe we're doing this," Archer said under his breath as we took the long narrow lane that led to Klausland. "We're breaking in. We've got to return a penguin without anyone seeing us. We're going to get lost. We'll call out the wrong password. The sprinklers will come on. We'll have to sit on the bus soaking wet. Shall I go on?"

"Archer," I said, keeping my voice to a whisper. "Aren't you sick of being told what to do, even when you're trying to do something good? We're *not* returning Sue. She needs to be set free from the Klauses. All the penguins do."

Sue was already trembling as we turned the corner to find the giant angels floating above us and the bazillion fairy lights twinkling in the trees. She knew exactly where we were.

"And how are you planning to set them all free?" Archer said. "Why can't we just pop Sue back, say goodbye and run for our lives?"

"Sue needs us!" I insisted. "*All* the penguins need us!"

"This place has security, Holly!" Archer darted behind a fir tree like a professional spy. "*Actual* security. There are cameras and barriers and passes. The Klauses want to keep people out. Not merrily let kids on to their property to steal their penguins!"

"Did you know that Sue doesn't like the cold?" I said,

running to catch up with him. "That's why I found her beside the school ovens earlier today. And that's why she doesn't like it here. She wants to be warm."

As we reached the edge of the fir-tree woods, Archer goggled at the Klauses' mansion. "But look at this place!" he said, flattening himself against a tree trunk and pointing towards the snow fountains and ice rink. "It's a penguin paradise!"

Sue's flipper slipped from my hand as she followed Archer's lead and hid behind a tree.

"It's not a paradise for Sue," I said, wondering if we could give all the penguins little elf hats and guide them out of Klausland, follow-my-leader style. "And something tells me the other penguins don't like it either. The Klauses built all of this for their own amusement. To keep *themselves* entertained. All they do is –"

From the dark woods ahead, a bright yellow light shot into my eyes and momentarily blinded me.

"Stop right there!" an angry voice shouted. "You're under arrest!"

THE INVITATION 21

"Under a vest?" I shouted, covering my eyes with my hands. "But I'm not wearing a vest."

"ARREST," the voice said again, this time sounding a little more high-pitched and a little less threatening. "It means you're in trouble and Father will call the police and Mother will give us presents for catching criminals."

Archer turned so pale, I thought he might pass out. "Quick, Holly," he said. "What was that password thingy? We need saving! Holly Folly Tolly! Yolly Nolly Jolly! Rolly Golly Wally!"

Setti and Toby appeared from the bushes with binoculars hung around their necks and torches attached to tinselled tool belts.

"Who are you calling a wally?" Toby flicked his torch off and on with an angry scowl. "You two are going to the top of the naughty list! Breaking on to our property. Calling us wallies. Sabotaging our plans to become the Most Festive Family."

"Toby's right," Setti said, looking us up and down as though we'd just crawled out of a stinky sewer. "Tell us what you're doing right now or I'll . . . I'll scream!"

"I just wanted to show Archer your lights," I said, holding my hands up as if Setti had a gun pointed at my chest. "Didn't I, Arch? I told him they were ice-credible. Tinseltastic. Elfmazing."

Setti curled her top lip and folded her arms across her chest. "Don't waste your breath, Carroll."

"Yeah," Toby added. "Tell us something we don't already know."

Archer looked at me as if to say, *Wow, they really are horri-bauble!* "Well, I guess I've seen the lights," he said. "We should really be getting home now."

"Not yet, Arch," I said, wondering where in Klausland Sue had got to. "I, umm . . . think I've lost something."

"Your sanity?" Setti laughed, tossing her hair off her shoulder and displaying a bright red poinsettia behind her ear. "Face it, Holly. No one in their right mind would go up against us in a Christmas competition. We're unbeatable."

"Yeah," Toby said after Setti had elbowed him in the ribs. "We're unbeatable. Unstoppable. Invincible."

"Children," a voice squealed. "Who are you talking to?"

My heart skipped a beat as Mr and Mrs Klaus walked through a clearing in the trees with their chins in the air. They were dressed in matching silk pyjamas and fur robes, and swigged cinnamon-smelling drinks from the tiniest cups and saucers I'd ever seen. I heard a tiny peep from the trees and disguised it as another fart. Where *was* that penguin?

"Mother!" Setti cried in the same squealy piglet tone as her mum. "Father! Holly Carroll and her accomplice

have been sneaking around the grounds. We caught them so we deserve a reward. I'd like a pink pony. One with –"

As I scanned the trees for Sue, I heard Setti mention something about crystal eyes, real silk hair, and making the pony fly with reindeer magic.

"Enough," Mrs Klaus snapped, patting her plaited hair, which had been moulded into the shape of a sleigh on top of her head. "Present pitches are scheduled for

Thursday, Poinsettia. I don't want to hear any more about gifts until then."

"But what about –"

"We don't want to hear about *anything* until then," Mr Klaus said with a firm gaze.

Setti fell silent and looked at the ground. Toby hid behind her.

"Well then!" Mrs Klaus beamed at me, transforming her face with a quick shake of her head. "Holly Carroll, I see you couldn't keep away. Did you want to show your friend here the rest of Klausland?"

I nodded as my heart pounded inside my ears.

"We don't have time for a tour today, I'm afraid," said Mr Klaus. "But what about this Friday? At our Hallomas party? You must bring your friend and the whole family."

He pulled a card from the inside of his robe and presented it to Archer.

"Hallomas?" Archer's fingers shook as he tried to open the envelope. "Like a mix between Halloween and Christmas?"

"Precisely," Mr and Mrs Klaus said together.

"Every day is an excuse to celebrate Christmas." Mr Klaus smiled with his blindingly white teeth. "Even Halloween. Wouldn't you agree, little girl?"

Archer held out the diamond-encrusted card for me to look at. "Holly," he murmured, showing me the sleigh filled with pumpkin-shaped presents on the front. "These guys are *good*."

Urgh. I didn't want to admit it, but Archer was right. The Klauses were cheerfully terrifying and I was scared of what they might come up with next.

"So we'll add you to the guest list?" Mrs Klaus said, tapping her foot.

"It's fancy dress," Mr Klaus added, walking back towards the house. "Christmas fancy dress, obviously."

"We'll be there," I said, trying to steady my quivering voice. "With bells on."

"We wouldn't expect anything less," Mr Klaus said.

As soon as the Klauses reached the ice fountains and

were out of sight, I ran around the trees, frantically searching for Sue. I'd only been searching for a moment or two when . . .

"What do we have here?" a voice said, followed by a panicked peeping noise. "Have you run away from the Ice Quarter again?"

I yanked Archer behind a holly bush and pointed at the Klauses' elf butler. "It's the Elfler!" I gasped. "He pops up everywhere."

"I can see why they call you a nuisance!" the Elfler said, carrying Sue around the side of the house and almost losing his balance on the mirrored ground. "We'll have to build a wall around the ice rink so you don't get yourself into any more trouble."

Within seconds, Sue and the Elfler disappeared into the darkness. All the energy drained from my body.

"What do we do now?" Archer said as we crept out of the trees and stared at the sparkling house. "Are we actually going to go to the Hallomas party?"

I nodded. If Mum and Dad saw the Klauses enjoying

Halloween, they might realise that it was OK to like more than just Christmas. Or it might convince them to let *me* celebrate Halloween with my friends. I crossed my fingers and took a deep breath, ack-noel-edging for the first time just how much I wanted to go to the Halloween Haunt.

"At least we'll be invited to Candy Cane Lane this time," Archer said as we walked back down the winding driveway. "And we won't need to draw any attention to ourselves."

I made a mental note of where all the security cameras were and grinned. "That's what you think!" I said. "We still need to rescue the penguins."

NEXT-LEVEL CHRISTMAS

22

On Wednesday, we added so many lights to our house, you couldn't see a millimetre of space. It was like the bricks and windows had been swallowed by fairy lights (or attacked by a billion house-eating fireflies, whichever you think sounds more impressive). Dad even added a runway to the roof and an inflatable penguin wearing a hi-vis vest so Santa could have a clear landing on Christmas Eve.

"That'll show them we're always thinking of others," Dad said, ticking it off his *101 Ways To Impress* The Christmas Chronicle *Editor* list. He also asked me to make slippers for the reindeer so they could rest their hooves while Santa delivered his presents, and while I'd normally think that was a tinselriffic idea, all I wanted to do was design a costume for the Hallomas party that could hide a family of penguins inside.

It was quite exciting, you know, this Hallomas thing. I didn't want to dive straight in or anything. It was more a quick toe dip to see how icy the waters were, but the more I thought about it, the more I found myself counting down the hours until we went. I made a Christmas wish that Mum and Dad would feel the same.

On Thursday before school, Mum ~~trapped me inside~~ asked me to join her in her studio where she was making new cushions, quilts and curtains for every room in the house. She even sprayed them with a pine and cranberry scent she'd mixed in the bathtub the day before. I was in charge of bottling the leftover 'Cheer Spray' to give to the parents at school.

Between bottling liquid in even amounts, making labels out of glitter, felt tips and the back of old Christmas cards, and writing wishes of cheer on to tags in my ~~quickest~~ neatest handwriting, I only just had enough time to eat my breakfast, chuck some leftovers out of the window for Reggie (who was in a MAJOR huff because I'd barely seen him all week), and put a fresh pair of candy-cane socks to christmafy my school uniform.. There was no time for learning the monster dance on YouTube that Liena had told me about, no time for trying out the sparkly spiderweb hairdo I'd dreamed up, and no time for finishing my maths homework – although I wasn't exactly upset about that one.

Things didn't get any calmer at school when Alice invited me to her house for a sleepover.

"Liena and I are going to make spooky signs to direct people to the Halloween Haunt," she said. "And we wanted to put black and red tinsel around the edges. Do you have any?"

"Do I have any *tinsel*?" I laughed. "Only one hundred and fifty-six boxes! I can ask Dad to grab some for me. He built a Tinsel Travelator in the attic so we could get to them easily, but it moves so fast I get travel sick."

Alice and Liena giggled. "Does that mean he said you can come to the Halloween Haunt?" Liena asked.

I shook my head. "Not yet," I said. "But I'm going to ask again. SUPER nicely. I'm going to be so Christmassy and jolly and cheerful, he won't be able to say n–!"

The Jolly Jeep screeched around the corner and skidded to a stop beside us.

"Holly!" Dad bawled through the window. "Come quick. Come quick. We've got another chrisaster!"

"What happened?" I said, climbing into the car to check that he was OK.

"The oven has broken!" Dad cried. He yanked my seat belt around me, leaned over to pull the door shut, and sped off before I had a chance to say goodbye to Alice and Liena. "THE. OVEN. HAS. BROKEN!"

He skidded around corners in a way that reminded me of that time we tried sledding down the stairs and I rolled head first into a radiator.

"I need my oven, Hols. It's a part of my soul. Can

you help me fix it?"

"But Alice invited me to hers tonight!" I said, clinging on to the edge of my seat. "We're going to make decorations for the Halloween Haunt. Which I really, REALLY want to go to!"

Dad's eyes grew so wide you would've thought I'd said a bad word like *Grinch* or *Scrooge* or *humbug*. "*Halloween decorations*? We've talked about this, Holly . . ."

"But it's just some arts and crafts!" I whined. "And loads of people from my class are going. They're going to make bunting and posters and backdrops for photos. They're even going to use tinsel!"

Dad's forehead wrinkled. "Hols, it really doesn't –"

"Aren't you a little bit curious to see how people use Halloween to spread cheer?" I said, wishing he'd stop panicking about his oven for two seconds and listen to me. "Because I am. All I'm asking is to go to Alice's house and help my friends prepare for a party. Maybe show off my skills with a glue gun and glitter stick. Or make some sparkly cobweb tablecloths. It's not exactly dangerous."

"Snowdrop, I'm not sure you –"

I couldn't help what happened next. The words sort of spilled out like that time I tried to fit eight mince pies in my mouth . . .

FEAR VS CHEER

23

"JUST BECAUSE YOU HATE HALLOWEEN DOESN'T MEAN I HAVE TO!" I shouted.

The car rolled to a stop at some traffic lights and several seconds of silence passed before Dad spoke.

"You think I hate Halloween?" he said eventually.

I stared at his worried eyes and sugar-coated cheeks. "Don't you?"

Dad shrugged. "I've never celebrated Halloween. And I don't really understand it. But do I *hate* it? No."

"So does that mean I can go to Alice's house and make some decorations for the Halloween Haunt?"

Dad turned the volume up on his Christmas carol playlist. "There's a lot to do tonight, Snowflake."

My shoulders slumped.

"But there's just over a week left until the editor from *The Christmas Chronicle* visits. If we can get everything done in time, maybe you can go to Alice's house another night?"

I gasped. Had I actually convinced Dad to let me do something that had nothing to do with Christmas? Had Nick Carroll, the most un-Halloweeny person on the planet, agreed to let me make decorations that spread fear, not cheer?

I stared out of the window, excitement building in my belly. Would we listen to spooky music? Should I write Halloween cards instead of Christmas cards? Was I meant to shout 'trick or treat' or 'trickle sweet'? I could hear Dad reeling off his list of plans for the editor, but I was too busy practising zombie faces in the reflection of the window to notice.

"– so you'll make the WLCC," Dad shouted over the Christmas carols. "And I'll –"

I jerked my head as Dad parked the car. "What's the

WLCC?" I said, stepping on to the pavement.

"The World's Largest Christmas Cracker," Dad said, scurrying to the boot of the car and handing me a huge box of pipes and cables for the oven. "The christmassiest Christmas cracker that's ever been invented. You're up to the challenge, right?"

As I stumbled towards the house, weighed down by my Hollyhood, Backpack of Cheer and the giant box of oven parts, I wondered if I could spend the evening carving a family of pumpkins instead of inventing something as useless as the –

Wait. What was I saying? *Nothing* to do with Christmas was useless. Especially the World's Largest Christmas Cracker. Just imagine how much cheer that could spread!

My head filled with fuzzy thoughts and unfamiliar feelings. I didn't know what to think. Did I love Christmas? Yes. Did I want to help Mum and Dad win the Most Festive Family competition? Yes. Would it all be a waste of time? Maybe. Would they notice if I slipped off to Alice's house? Most definitely. Should I do it anyway?

Ummm . . .

I thought about making Halloween signs with Alice, hanging out with Archer, and fashionising a mask for the Halloween Haunt. If I hadn't been invited to any of those things, I wouldn't be thinking twice about creating the WLCC. But I *had* been invited, and that was special, too. Wasn't it?

I had almost made it to the front door when I heard a loud 'HEE-HAW!', followed by stampeding hooves and heavy panting.

Reggie sprinted towards me. His slobbery tongue flopped out of his mouth and every few steps he'd leap into the air and close his eyes. In those few brief seconds, I think he imagined he was soaring over the garden and rising high above the rooftops – but the truth was, he was struggling to get his front legs off the ground and he very nearly ran head first into a holly bush.

"Reggie!" I cried, dropping the oven supplies on the ground. "You've got to be careful!"

Reggie opened his eyes, realised his hooves were

still on the ground and skidded to a halt.

"Hee-haw?" he brayed sadly.

I wrapped my arms around his neck. "I'm really proud of you for trying to fly, Reg," I said, stroking his rough mane. "But you do know that it might not happen?"

Reggie tilted his head as if he was asking a question.

"It's not that I don't believe in you, or don't think you have the talent," I said, trying my hardest not to offend him. "But you don't live at the North Pole. You don't have Santa's magic. And you're not a real r–"

Reggie's shoulders bristled.

"No, no," I said quickly, waving my

hands in the air. "That's not what I meant."

But it was too late. Reggie knew what I had been about to say and it had hit him like an icicle to the heart. He turned away from me.

"I just meant that you're not *ready* yet," I said. "I bet it takes Santa's reindeer years to learn how to fly. You've only been trying for a few weeks. I'm . . . I'm sorry if I said the wrong thing."

Hesitantly, Reggie rested his head on my shoulder.

Phew. I was *not* used to upsetting people, and the very thought of hurting someone's feelings made me feel sick. Especially someone I loved as much as Reggie.

As I hugged Reggie as tight as I could, I thought about Mum and Dad, and how much the Halloween Haunt would upset them. I could just picture Dad's disappointed eyes and Mum's wobbling bottom lip. Their cheer-o-meter ratings would plummet to a two or maybe even a ONE, and the thought of them losing their cheer completely was too difficult to imagine.

It was in that moment I realised I was going to have

to forget about going to Alice's house and the Halloween Haunt (for now) and go along with their plans to out-Christmas the Klauses. Putting my feelings aside was the right thing to do. The Christmassy thing to do.

Right?

THE CHRISTMAS HELPER

24

The Klauses' Hallomas party arrived faster than the time it took for Dad to demolish a freshly decorated grotto cake.

"Daaaaad," I called, already yawning after a long week of school, Christmas crafts and house decorating. "Mum said it's time to get into our Hallomas costumes."

"Not now, Hols!" Dad yelled back. "These fountains won't fill themselves."

I walked out of the house to find Dad kneeling inside a makeshift fountain that he'd built out of wooden crates, plastic sheets and a couple of rusty pipes.

"The Klauses can keep their ice fountains!" he

said with a screwdriver behind his ear and a wrench wedged under his armpit. "We're going to have drink fountains with real hot chocolate, eggnog and mulled wine overflowing into three layers of special, secret ingredients. I'm calling them refreshmas fountains."

"Is it, er, *safe*?" I asked, noticing one of the pipes was a bit bent and had a hole in the middle.

"I'm going to build a roof over the top," Dad continued, making a rainbow shape with his arm. "And Snow will design some special cups so the neighbours can help themselves to drinks when they pass. They'll all be kept at just the right temperature, and we'll have a station over here for toppings and syrups and cinnamon straws."

He dived head first into the biggest fountain and started muttering to himself about loose connections. He was basically frantical (a mix between being frantic and hysterical) – a bit like Santa might be if he fell asleep on Christmas Eve and only had an hour left to deliver all the presents. I'd never seen Dad like that before. He was acting like the world might end if he didn't finish his precious fountains. Like the house might come tumbling down if we didn't win the Most Festive Family competition. Like he would never forgive himself if he didn't prove he loved Christmas more than anyone else in the world.

I totally understood why Dad loved Christmas so much. We were the Christmas family that spread cheer all year, and it brought us more joy than anything. But I was starting to wonder if Dad had ever enjoyed anything else. Had he tried skateboarding? Or eaten fish and chips out of a paper bag? Or spent the day watching movies without mentioning Christmas or Santa once?

"Dad?" I said, climbing into the fountain and putting my hand on his shoulder. "I know this is all important to you, but . . ." I paused, unsure if I really wanted to know the answer. *"Why?"*

Dad stopped screwing bolts into the ground and took a deep breath. Gradually, his heavy breathing slowed and his shoulders slumped. He sat down, leaning against the fountain and curled his knees to his chest.

"My parents were the hardest-working people I'd ever known," he said, staring into the distance. "We came from Jamaica when I was two years old and they did everything they could to provide for me and my seven brothers and sisters. They worked two jobs each, sometimes three, and they expected the same hard work and dedication from all of us."

"So that's why you work so hard?" I said.

"Not exactly," Dad said. "My mum and dad were never happier than when one of us came home with an award or certificate or top marks in an exam. They'd shower us with praise and hugs and make special meals with our favourite foods."

Dad's mouth was practically salivating at the thought of the delicious food his parents used to cook for him.

"But I was never very good academically," he went on. "My grades were poor and I always felt like I got less attention than everyone else. Until one Christmas Eve. My mum – your gram gram – broke her arm and couldn't make her famous cocoa tea. Every Christmas

Eve she'd spend hours slowly stirring it in a pot on the stove. She'd turn the heat down low, add some secret ingredients, and fill the house with the smell of cinnamon, the sound of Jamaican Christmas carols, and that indescribable festive feeling. It was the one night of the year she'd let us stay up late and watch Christmas movies until the last drop of cocoa tea was gone. It was one of her Christmas traditions she loved the most."

"So what happened when Gram Gram couldn't make her tea?" I asked, sitting down beside him.

Dad wrapped his arm around me. "When I saw how upset and

in pain she was, I emptied the kitchen cupboards and made a self-stirring spoon out of an electric whisk, an old ladle and one of my toy cars that whizzed around the rim of the pot." He laughed. "You should have seen her face when she came home from hospital! Her arm was wrapped in a thick blue cast, she had a sling tied around her neck and it looked like she hadn't slept in days. But despite all that, she looked more surprised – no – *elated* than I'd ever seen her. It was like I'd saved Christmas."

"Oh wow!"

"She didn't stop praising me all night," Dad went on. "We played games and watched movies until gone midnight, and everyone cheered my name when I handed out mugs full of cocoa tea. They said it was the best drink they'd ever tasted!"

He sighed happily. "I made a new invention every day while her arm was in a sling. I soon felt what it was like to do something good for someone else. That fizzy, proud, excited feeling is something I couldn't describe.

But then my mum's arm healed and she didn't need me as much. The one time she did need me –"

"Was Christmas?" I said.

Dad nodded. "My mum and dad wanted to give us the Christmas they never had. They worked night shifts, took on more hours and only had Christmas Day off to celebrate. So I decided to step up."

"How?"

"During the summer holidays and half-terms, I'd make our own family wrapping paper," Dad said. "I'd organise a family photo for our Christmas cards and try out new Christmas recipes. My mum and dad were so grateful, they stopped worrying about my poor grades or empty spaces on the trophy shelf, and praised me for my creativity and helpfulness instead. I finally had the attention I'd craved from them." He paused. "It became quite addictive, to tell you the truth."

"So that's why you love Christmas so much?" I asked.

Dad's gaze suddenly hardened. "And that's why we can't lose to the Klauses," he said sternly. "I don't like disappointing people."

"You wouldn't be disappointing us, Dad!" I said.

"Maybe not," he said, looking at his reindeer antler trainers. "But I'd be disappointing myself."

It was strange to hear that Dad had had a life before Mum, me and Ivy and our house on Sleigh Ride Avenue. But I finally understood why this all meant so much to him. Gram Gram and Gramps may have moved back to Jamaica before I was born, but Dad still wanted that same level of satisfaction. That same 'fizzy, proud, excited' feeling he'd mentioned earlier. It was sort of how I felt when Archer made me a friendship scarf and when Alice invited me to her house for a sleepover. It was that feeling of being wanted.

"Dad?" I said. "Did you have any friends when you were growing up?"

"Of course!" Dad said, as if it were the most obvious question in the world. "I had seven brothers and sisters! They were the best friends anyone could ask for. Even if they did wreck my train set."

"But what about doing things outside of Christmas and your family? Did you find joy in anything else?"

Dad looked confused. "I didn't need anything else, Hols," he said. "My family were my friends and they were the best friends ever. Why would I need anything more?"

Dad climbed out of the fountain, picked up a paintbrush and started painting the outside. Reggie poked his head around the side of the house and opened his eyes wide as if to say, "Flying practice?"

"Not now, Reggie," I mouthed.

As Mum came to the door and reminded us there was 'snow time to lose' and we had to leave for the Hallomas party in ten minutes' time, I couldn't help wondering if I was going to follow in Dad's footsteps. Was I destined for a life of constant Christmas crafts and hours of inventing? Was I going to have a totally friendless future?

Did I really want to be obsessed with *just* Christmas for the rest of my life?

THE CHRISTMAS COSTUMES

25

"Come on! Come on!" Mum shouted, darting across the kitchen to grab one more box of mince pies for the road. "We can't be late!"

"Snooooooow!" Dad yelped, being dragged behind Mum in their home-made joined-up reindeer Hallomas costumes. "Remember we're attached –"

Mum heaved the fridge open just as Dad came up behind her and headbutted the door.

"SHRIEKING SLEIGH BELLS!" he yelled, clutching his forehead. "How can you make these costumes and forget that we're connected?"

He rubbed his head and guided Mum into the hallway,

where Archer, Ivy and I were waiting beside the open front door.

"These costumes are amazing!" I said, jumping up and down in excitement. "I asked Alice about fancy-dress parties and she said that the costumes don't always have to be scary. You just have to dress up as someone or something different and then see if other people know who you are. We might even have a chance at winning the costume competition if they have one!"

"In that case," Dad said, waving the Christmacam in the air, "we should have a photo before we go!"

Archer obediently posed like a flying reindeer. He was such a good sport. Mum hadn't really given him much of a choice when she'd sped out of her studio and shoved one third of a reindeer trio costume over his head. He just took one look at the brown fur, the red nose, the antler headband and fluffy hoof slippers and said, "Cool costume, Mrs C."

I'm not entirely sure that 'cool' was the right word. 'Boiling-hot sweaty mess' was probably more accurate.

But Dad hadn't had time to make the miniature ice fans he'd planned to hide inside the hoods, so we just had to put up with feeling like tightly wrapped turkeys roasting in an oven.

Like Mum and Dad's costume, Archer and I were also connected. I was one reindeer, Archer was another, and there was a third stuffed reindeer standing on its hind legs between us. Mum and Dad had an extra stuffed reindeer between them, too, a bit like reindeers doing the can-can.

"Why be one reindeer when you can be three?" Mum smiled. "That's THREE times the cheer."

Mum and Dad *were* getting a bit carried away with the whole trying to out-cheer the Klauses thing. Just because they wore three Santa hats instead of one, or played carols twice as loud, or baked four times the number of mince pies as they had the day before, that didn't necessarily mean they were spreading any more cheer, did it?

"OK, everyone," Dad said, preparing to take an elfie of us all. "Say Merry Christmas!"

"MERRY CHRIS–"

"WAIT!" Mum cried.

"What?" Dad said, swatting the stuffed reindeer's antlers out of his face. "What's wrong?"

Mum pointed her finger at me, Archer and the third reindeer between us, and then at herself, Dad, the reindeer between them, and Ivy, who was perched on Mum's hip in a tiny reindeer costume of her own. "Santa has *eight* reindeer," she gasped. "But we only make seven! Where's the eighth reindeer? *Where's the eighth reindeer?*"

"You're right!" Dad gasped. "Where are we going to find an eighth reindeer at this hour?"

Suddenly the front door burst open, a rush of cool air filled the corridor, and the setting sun illuminated a wide figure that filled the door frame.

After pausing for dramatic effect, Reggie strutted in, lifting his legs high and shaking his mane as if he'd just had a fresh blow-dry. As his hooves clip-clopped against the wooden floor, his fluffy bum swung from side to side and he shot us a wonky grin, complete with a raised eyebrow and slight lip-curl.

"REGGIE!" I cheered.

Reggie tilted his head, raised his chin and changed poses every few seconds. He was in his element! In fact, I wasn't sure what Reggie wanted more – to fly Santa's sleigh on Christmas Eve or be the first animal to grace the cover of *Vogue* magazine. He was born to be in front of the camera.

After a few clicks of the Christmacam, Dad adjusted Reggie's inflatable antlers and patted him on the back.

"Well, folks," he said, ignoring the excited farts puffing from Reggie's bum. "I think we've found our eighth reindeer!"

What do you think was the first thing we noticed when we arrived at the Hallomas party? The piles of white and silver pumpkins covered in glitter and stacked up almost as high as the house? Nope. The photographers in zombie elf costumes? Think again. The carol singers telling ghost stories around a campfire? Not even close.

"Carrolls!" Mrs Klaus sang, walking out of the front door with her arms wide. "What in fake fur are you wearing?"

Mum's mouth practically hit the floor when she saw Mrs Klaus's outfit. "Your dress," she said, taking in the bazillion bejewelled layers of tulle and fur. "It's . . . it's . . ."

"I know," Mrs Klaus said, spinning around with one arm in the air and the other on her hip. "The train was a little too short for my liking and I demanded the designer find more rubies for the neckline, but I think it's just about festive enough."

"You look *tinseltastic*," Mum breathed, her eyes going all goggly like a surprised frog. "But I thought it was a fancy-dress party?"

Mrs Klaus's eyes narrowed. "Do I not look *fancy* to you?" she said tartly.

"Oh," Mum said, her voice going up a few decibels as her whole face turned red. "Of course! You're the fanciest. The prettiest. The . . ."

"Vainest?" I whispered to Archer.

Archer smirked as Mrs Klaus patted her hair, which had been plaited and shaped to look like an ornate Christmas tree. It even had gold tinsel woven into it and tiny pumpkin baubles hanging off the edges.

"I must say," Dad said, looking at the spiderweb-covered ice fountains. "I wasn't sure about a Hallomas party at first, but it's quite clever, isn't it? It's not really Halloween at all. It's more like saying 'hallo' to Christmas. Like we're greeting it with open arms."

"The word I believe you're looking for, Nick, is *inventive*," Mr Klaus said, walking out of the house in a candy-cane tuxedo with glistening spider buttons. He draped his arm around Mrs Klaus's shoulder.

"Khris is right," Mrs Klaus said, patting her husband's hand and then pushing it off her shoulder in case it creased her dress. "We're certainly known for our creativity and clever inventions, but we don't like to brag."

I let out a *pfft* sound that I had to disguise as a hiccup.

"Anyway," Mrs Klaus continued. "It looks like you may have *misunderstood* the dress code, Carrolls. Might you be more comfortable enjoying the celebrations outside where fewer people will see you?"

"I don't think so," Dad said. "We can spread cheer however we look. Right, Reggie?"

Reggie let out a loud 'hee-haw!' and clip-clopped his hooves in excitement.

"Yes, well," Mrs Klaus said, her jaw clenched. "I'm afraid I must draw the line at . . ." She looked at Reggie in disgust. "*Pets.*"

"That's OK," Dad said, refusing to let the Klauses get the upper hand. "This one's great at making friends inside or out. Off you go, Reg."

Reggie trotted off after a photographer who'd walked past with two cameras around his neck and another in his hands.

"Hee-haw!" Reggie brayed as he nipped the photographer's heels to get him to take his photo.

"Make sure you get his wonky eye!" I shouted. "That's his good side!"

THE HALLOMAS PARTY

26

D ad beamed at the Klauses. "Reggie will be the life and soul of the party in no time," he said.

Mrs Klaus glared at Dad with as much festive cheer as a mouldy potato. "Let's hope he doesn't hog *too* much attention," she said sharply. "It's not polite to steal the limelight at someone else's party."

Mum's cheeks were so red, they looked like they were on fire. "I'm terribly, utterly, toe-toe-totally sorry we turned up like this, Laina," she said in her fake posh accent. "We thought a fancy-dress party meant that we had to wear costumes. Truth be told, we haven't been to a Halloween party before. Or many parties at all, for that matter. We're not quite sure of the . . . what word would you use? Air-tee-kit?"

"Etiquette," Mrs Klaus said in a chilly voice.

"Well, I like them," Dad said stoutly. "You worked day and night on these costumes, Snow. We might as well show them off!" He did a little jig that tore a tiny hole in the seam and made me and Ivy giggle.

"Home-made?" Mrs Klaus said, almost wincing. "I might've guessed."

Before she could throw any more not-so-subtle insults at us, a row of shiny red sports cars and black limousines circled the spooky snow fountains and sent Mrs Klaus into a tizzy.

"EUGENE!" she shrieked, pulling a tiny bell from her sleeve and tinkling it above her head. The Elfler hurried over, his expression as cheerless as ever. "Show the Carrolls to the dining hall. A quiet spot at the back, perhaps?"

The Elfler bowed and guided us towards the house.

"And remember there are no children in the ballroom tonight, Eugene," Mrs Klaus shouted after us. "Find

Setti and Toby and ask them to watch those three." She pointed towards me, Archer and Ivy, and then turned back around and threw her arms out as if she were performing on stage in front of ten thousand people.

"CLAUDIA!" she squealed. "ERNEST! How spooktacular to see you."

Mum looked at Mrs Klaus in awe and tripped up the steps as Dad yanked her through the doorway.

"Nick!" she cried. "Watch where you're go— oh!"

The room we stood in was almost as big as the hall at school. With bright white walls and a mirrored ceiling, it looked like we were trapped in a never-ending igloo. There was a sweeping staircase with candy-cane spindles and at least fifty giant, crystallised candy canes hanging from the ceiling. Everything from the floor to the staircase was covered in thin silky cobwebs, and a huge white piano in the centre of the room had the lid propped open and a wave of candy canes and silver pumpkins cascading out.

"And I thought I had a sweet tooth!" Dad said,

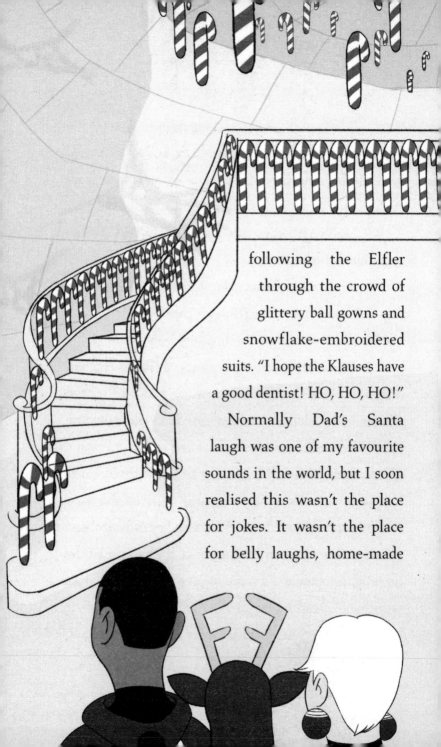

following the Elfler through the crowd of glittery ball gowns and snowflake-embroidered suits. "I hope the Klauses have a good dentist! HO, HO, HO!"

Normally Dad's Santa laugh was one of my favourite sounds in the world, but I soon realised this wasn't the place for jokes. It wasn't the place for belly laughs, home-made

costumes or having any
fun at all, it seemed.
Everyone at this party
had just turned up to
look good, to show off
their sports car or diamond
necklace or thick bushy moustache that looked like the
matted fur on Reggie's bum.

We didn't have a single thing to show off. Nobody
wanted to hear about Dad's latest inventions. A group
of women scoffed when Mum told them about her
award-winning apron business. And when I tried to

show everyone my funky nutcracker dance, the Elfler escorted me into the empty corridor quicker than you could say, 'Season's Greetings'.

"OK," he said, wiping his brow as he hurried Archer, Ivy and me to the end of a long, deserted hallway. "This is the Tree or Treat Room. Please remain here until you are collected. Have all the treats you like, but please don't touch the presents under the trees. We know exactly how many are there, and the Klauses will know if one goes missing."

"The Tree or Treat Room?" Archer whispered. "Like 'trick or treat'?"

I shrugged my shoulders. "I've never heard of it," I said. "Do you think it'll be fun?"

"Anything's more fun than being stuck in that bright white room with the fancy music," Archer replied. "And I think this one has sweets, so it can't be that bad."

Cautiously, Archer put his hand on the door and pushed it open. What were we going to find on the other side?

Children playing party games? A disco? A fountain of sweets and giant trampolines?

THE TREE OR TREAT ROOM

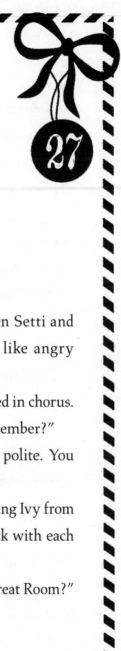

27

The doors had barely opened when Setti and Toby popped up in front of us like angry jack-in-the-boxes.

"What are *you* doing here?" they whined in chorus.

"Your parents invited us," I said. "Remember?"

Toby laughed. "They were just being polite. You weren't actually *supposed* to come."

"Well, we're here now," Archer said, taking Ivy from me to give my arms a rest. "So we're stuck with each other for a few hours."

"Stuck with each other? In *our* Tree or Treat Room?" Setti screeched.

"Absolutely not! You'll steal our presents," Toby shouted.

"You'll ruin our trees."

"You'll –"

"Be leaving soon," I said plainly. "Honestly, we're not here to ruin or steal anything . . ." (OK, OK, except Sue and the other penguins, but we'd be *freeing*, not stealing them. There was a big difference.) "I don't know why you're so . . . so . . ."

"So what?" Toby said, his face turning red.

"Choose your words carefully, Carroll," Setti added.

I looked from Setti's icy scowl to Toby's exaggerated pout. "I don't know why you're so worried about us," I said. "You're easily going to win the Most Festive Family competition. You've got everything anyone could dream of. My mum is in total awe of you, my dad has never felt so out-cheered, and if you ask me, I think you've already won."

Setti's shoulders relaxed as a grin spread across Toby's face.

"Don't be so hard on yourself, Hols," Archer said, letting Ivy play with his antlers. "You're the Christmas Carrolls! You've spread more cheer than anyone I know."

Archer really was the best friend anyone could ask for. "That's nice, Arch," I said, smiling. "But they've got a Tree or Treat Room, for goodness' sake! What even is that?"

"You haven't heard of our famous Tree or Treat Room?" Toby said, standing aside so we could see the enormous, glittering room in all its glory. "This is our smallest festive function room. Mother and Father use it for something different every month. During October, it becomes the Tree or Treat Room, just in time for the Hallomas party."

The room in front of us was long and wide, with golden walls and bright red carpet. Tree-shaped chandeliers hung from the tall ceilings and plush green curtains hung around windows that looked out on to the snowy mountain behind the house. Twenty-five towering trees were evenly spaced around the room, each one decorated with so many ornaments and lights and candy canes, you could barely see the branches.

"Every guest has to bring a decoration for a tree or a treat to go underneath," Setti explained, walking us around the room so she could keep her beady eyes on us. "It's a way to thank Mother and Father for putting on such a wonderful party."

"It's polite to give your hosts a gift," Toby added.

"Yeah, sooooo . . ." Setti and Toby put their hands out and wagged their fingers like impatient toddlers.

"A gift?" I said. "For a party? Of course. Umm . . ."

I patted down my reindeer costume, wondering what I could muster up. A handful of fur? A piece of antler?

"Here," Archer said, reaching inside his reindeer hood and pulling out some crinkled paper. "I made this for Holly, but I can always make another one."

He handed the booklet to Setti, who turned it over in her hands. "Carols?" she said, reading Archer's scribbly handwriting on the front. "You're giving the Carrolls some carols?"

"It's just a little gift," Archer said, turning red. "Holly and her family helped my friends last month and I've been trying to think of ways to thank them. I know they like to sing carols in the garden each morning, so I thought I'd write them some new ones."

"Archer!" I whispered, my eyes filling with tears. "That's . . . that's . . ."

"I can write you some others," he said. "If you want. I actually kind of enjoyed it."

Setti and Toby stared at Archer like they were holding back tears, swallowing laughs or about to let out equally stinky farts.

"Oh," Setti said. "That's actually quite . . ."

I looked at her expectantly.

Toby laughed. "Pathetic? Rude? Cheap?"

"I was going to say pointless," Setti said, chucking the booklet under a tree. "Mother asks the London Symphony Orchestra to record a different carol for us each year. We don't waste time singing our own."

My mouth dropped open. "There's no need to be

cruel," I said, watching Archer's smile fade. "We didn't know about the Tree or Treat Room, OK? We didn't know we had to bring a gift."

Setti smiled spitefully. "But I thought you were always prepared to spread cheer?"

Wow. She had me there.

"I think they were too busy making those repulsive costumes to think about spreading cheer," Toby said.

Archer's eyebrows lifted so high, they disappeared under his hood. I was (for once) stunned to silence. Ivy started to cry.

"I think this is getting out of hand," Archer said, finding his voice again. "You don't need to –"

CRASH!

I jumped out of my ~~skin~~ fur as Setti and Toby raced to the window. Screams and shouts echoed across Klausland as bright white floodlights flashed and everyone ran outside from the main ballroom.

"What's going on?" I said, dragging Archer and Ivy across the room. "What's happened?"

Setti and Toby turned to look at me with bright red cheeks.

"It's a donkey," Toby said in horror. "A donkey is ruining everything!"

GAME ON

28

B y the time we'd made it outside and followed
everyone to the Ice Quarter, the penguins
were running in all directions, the ice bridge
had completely collapsed, cracks were zigzagging
through the surface of the ice lake, and Reggie was
huddled behind Mum and Dad, who looked like they
were about to be sick.

"Reggie's never done anything like this before," Dad
said, trying to calm his own wheezing breaths as much
as Reggie's. "He's a good reindeer. He just gets a little
overexcited. Doesn't he, Snow?"

"Yes, yes, quite," Mum said, as flustered as that time

she accidentally sewed her hand inside a home-made oven glove. "I can see we're in quite a bind."

"He didn't *mean* to break your ice rink," Dad said. "And I'm sure we can fix it."

"Ice rink?" Mrs Klaus gasped, resting her hand on her heart. "*Ice rink?* Khris, did you hear what he called our sparkle kingdom?"

Mr Klaus's cheeks reddened. "I'm not one for causing a scene, Mr Carroll, but you are clearly trying to make a mockery of Klausland *and* our Hallomas party and I just won't stand for it."

As the crowd swelled, so did the mutterings.

"You come in . . ." Mrs Klaus flinched, ". . . *costumes*. You try to hog the limelight. And you bring this CREATURE who terrifies our prestigious penguins, ruins the performance they've worked so hard on, and smashes our ice kingdom to smithereens. It's like you're trying to sabotage our chances at winning the Most Festive Family competition."

A collective gasp ran through the crowd.

"No, no, no," Mum said, her posh voice wavering. "You've got it all wrong, Laina."

"Ah, security!" Mr Klaus shouted, clicking his fingers above his head. "This way, chaps. Please escort the Carrolls back to the car. They'll be leaving now."

The security elf-ficer with the prickly moustache led a group of men and women (all dressed as Christmas soldiers) towards Mum and Dad. The crowd watched in anticipation.

"Mum! Dad!" I yelled, dragging Archer and Ivy with me as I ran over. "What happened?"

"I don't know!" Dad said helplessly as the security team edged nearer. "One minute I was telling a rather regal gentleman about the improvements I made to our carol-singing toilet, and the next, we heard this almighty crash, a screech that sounded like a wailing yeti, and everyone ran outside like the house was on fire."

"Reggie was already quivering in the corner when we arrived," Mum said. "But he couldn't have done all of this himself. He just *couldn't*."

I knelt down beside Reggie, forgetting that Archer and I were connected and pulling him down with me.

"What happened, boy?" I whispered, stroking his mane. "It's OK, I'm not angry. I know you didn't do this on purpose."

A tear ran down Reggie's nose. He motioned towards the ice bridge and then made a rainbow shape with his nose.

"You were walking along the bridge?" Archer said.

Reggie shook his head and tried again.

"You were . . . looking for rainbows?" Dad said.

Reggie repeated his actions in slow motion.

"OH!" I gasped, covering my mouth with my hand. "You were trying to fly?"

I could almost see it. The ice bridge was the perfect runway. A slippery surface. A bit of elevation. Something to leap off.

"Did you hurt yourself?" I said, checking him over for bumps or bruises.

Reggie shook his head as Archer and I hugged him harder than we'd ever hugged anyone.

"What shall we do with the penguins, madam?" a nutcracker soldier called, chasing a row of waddling penguins through the crowd. My heart leaped when I thought I spied Sue and her little blue sling, but there were so many penguins darting in every direction, I couldn't be sure.

Mrs Klaus squeezed the bridge of her nose with her fingertips and waved her other hand in the air.

"Put them in the ice caves," she muttered. "Or somewhere else they'll be out of sight."

"How are we going to free the penguins now?"

I hissed in Archer's ear. "Everyone's watching. The floodlights are on. There's security everywhere! We'll have to come back another time."

Archer groaned quietly. "Are you *still* thinking about that? This is their home, Holly. They belong to the Klauses."

"They *belong* wherever they are happy," I said stubbornly. "And that's not here!"

"Snow-K," Mr Klaus announced, pulling a cigar from his tuxedo pocket. "Let's not allow this little incident to ruin the festivities. Everyone back to the ballroom for monster mince pies and a few snowtacular scares!"

The crowd cheered and flowed back to the party, leaving us surrounded by nutcracker soldiers, the stony-faced Klauses, and half a dozen penguins skidding haphazardly across the broken ice.

"Laina," Mum said. "We are toe-toe-totally sorry. How can we ever make this up to you?"

Mrs Klaus forced a thin smile. "You can pull out of the competition?" she said. "Not that that will repair our sparkle kingdom or improve our Hallomas party, of course, but it's a start."

Dad made a face like he'd just eaten reindeer poop, Mum looked like she was going to pass out, and I think Reggie would've tackled Mrs Klaus to the ground if Archer hadn't held him back.

A few seconds of silence floated by. Dad took a deep and meaningful breath.

"I think it's time we went back to Sleigh Ride Avenue," he said. "We have some work to do before the editor from *The Christmas Chronicle* comes to visit."

Mrs Klaus stiffened. "You're . . . you're not pulling out then?"

"I'm afraid not," Mum said, adjusting her antlers. "We'd never give up on spreading cheer."

Mr and Mrs Klaus looked as if they'd just thrown up in their mouths.

"But I hope we can still be friends?" Mum added with a beam.

JUST BEING HONEST

29

I *needed a break from Christmas.*
   There.
   I said it.

It's not that I hated Christmas all of a sudden. That could *never* happen. But all this trying to out-Christmas the Klauses was getting tiring. Especially as we had more hope of winning the ice hockey in the Winter Olympics (but only if Reggie was in goal).

The days were slipping by, and all we were doing was making more Christmas cushions (which we now didn't have room for), practising the perfect roast turkey (which Dad had mastered by the age of ten) and adding more lights to the house (which was doing nothing but increasing the electricity bill and giving the neighbours a headache).

All I wanted was a break. I wanted to go to Alice's sleepover and tell ghost stories. I wanted to stay in a house that wasn't painted red and green, or had Christmas trees taking up every centimetre of every room. I wanted to read a book that wasn't about Christmas. I wanted to go to a café and order a cold lemonade instead of hot chocolate with marshmallows. I wanted to do something important and worthwhile, like stop the ice caps from melting in the Arctic or free the Klauses' dancing penguins! Was that so bad? To get away from the decorations and carols and Christmas jumpers . . . just for a while?

The journey home from the Klauses had been long and awkward, but it had given me loads of time to think about stuff. In particular, I'd thought about Dad. About how he'd spent his childhood trying to impress his parents and out-Christmas his siblings. About how he'd let his competitiveness turn into an obsession, and how that obsession became his life.

I loved Dad more than anything, but that wasn't how I wanted to turn out. I wanted to have *other* interests. I wanted to have *friends*. I wanted to experience *everything*. All the Christmassiness the world could offer, AND all the non-Christmas magic, too.

"HOLLY!" Dad shouted. "Are you listening?"

I snapped out of my trance. "Huh?"

It was Sunday morning, and we were all in Dad's garden workshop. "We'll add speakers around the front door so it sings to the editor when he arrives," Mum said, ticking ideas off a giant sheet of paper on the floor. "We'll host a Christmas concert in the street, complete with marching nutcrackers, a snowman choir and a breakdancing reindeer."

Reggie wiggled his eyebrows and spun on the floor with one hoof behind his head as if giving us a preview.

"Holly will find out what the editor likes to do in his spare time and make a hobby tree just for him," Mum went on.

"Hold on a second," I said. I should probably have listened to the whole conversation in case Mum had signed me up to do a marathon around Lapland or volunteered me to fly to the moon in Santa's sleigh (I wouldn't put either past her). "I don't have time to make an entire hobby tree in six days!"

Dad beamed. "With a little Christmas cheer, you can do anything you put your mind to, Snowflake!"

I gritted my teeth. "And how am I meant to find out what the editor's hobbies are?"

"Research!" Mum said, pulling three glue sticks and some broken Christmas bunting from her star-covered apron. "Use the internet. Write him a letter. Oooh, you could interview his parents!"

Archer stifled a laugh as Mum handed him one end of the bunting and hung the rest over his head while she wrestled with a stubborn glue-stick lid.

"And what about the Halloween Haunt?" I said, shooting my shot while they were in DHFM (deliriously happy festive mode). "If I make the hobby tree and do everything else you're asking me to do, will you let me go?"

My heart thudded as I waited for an answer.

"Yes, yes," Dad said, absent-mindedly dragging his latest decorvention into the workshop. "I don't see why not."

My body froze. Did I sleighriously hear that right? Should I get Dad to sign a contract? Record it somehow? Keep the proof that he said I could do something un-Christmassy and un-Carrolly and un–

"What did I tell you, Snow?" Dad shouted, pulling his head out of a ten-foot inflatable turkey. "THIS is the way to present our Christmas menu to the editor. It'll be like a treasure hunt!"

"Dad?" I said. "You know that the Halloween Haunt is on the same day as the editor's visit, right?"

"And we should fill the room with balloons!" Mum shouted with glee. "We can hang photos of the different puddings available, and that's how the editor can choose which one he'd like!"

I persevered. "Are you sure you're both OK with that? I mean, I'm really grateful and everything, but –"

"*Coo-ee!*" a voice shrilled from outside the workshop.

Mum and Dad finally stopped talking.

"That's not who I think it is, is it?" Archer said.

One by one we poked our heads around the corner of the workshop door.

"No," I said, my insides suddenly churning. "No, no, no, no, no."

"*We come bearing gifts!*"

Archer and I exchanged nervous glances.

"WHAT IN ROASTED CHESTNUTS ARE THE KLAUSES DOING HERE?" Dad yelled.

THE SURPRISE VISIT 30

The Klauses stood so still and silent, they could've been mistaken for life-size Christmas ornaments. Like a family of shiny porcelain dolls, they wore matching green blazers with swirly Ks embroidered on the pockets and tiny gold bells hanging off the collars. Mrs Klaus had fashioned her hair into a braided Christmas pudding, and Setti was wearing so many poinsettias on her headband, I wondered how she could hold her head up.

"We bring presents!" Mrs Klaus said, motioning towards the Elfler, who was holding a silver tray with a giant domed lid. "Won't you come and join us?"

Dad's eyebrow was already twitching. Mum smoothed down her apron and anxiously ran her fingers through her hair. Reggie let out a deep, almost-growling 'hee-haw'.

"They're inviting *us* to join *them*?" I said, shaking my head. "In our own house?"

"Maybe they've come to apologise, Snowflake," Mum said, already walking out to greet them. "Don't be so quick to judge."

"We wanted to check you were OK," Mrs Klaus shouted, her eyes darting from the house to the snow maze and back to Dad's workshop. "We feel we've been a little . . . how would you put it?"

Rude? Unwelcoming? Obnoxious?

"Unfair," Mr Klaus said, shrugging his shoulders like their behaviour was nothing more than a light-hearted joke. "Won't you come over and share some joy?"

"Of course!" Dad bellowed, running over to join Mum. "Let me show you our refreshmas fountains. I think you'll find them quite snowtacular!"

Hang on . . . Was Dad actually SHOWING the

Klauses his inventions? Did he *want* them to steal his ideas? Or had he suddenly realised we had no hope of winning, and was just going back to being good old 'spreading cheer throughout the year' Dad?

"Right then, children," Mr Klaus said, slicking his hair back with a thin golden comb in the shape of a sleigh. "Why don't you two run along with, er . . ."

He clicked his fingers at Archer and me.

"Holly," I said, raising my eyebrows. "HOL-LY."

"That's the one," he said with a grin, making his pointy chin even more prominent. "Play with Holly and her friend and we'll be back later."

Mrs Klaus put on her annoying tinkleless laugh and took the gift from the Elfler. "Don't forget this," she said, chucking some paper wrapped in green ribbon to Setti. "We wouldn't want the Carrolls to think we've turned up empty-handed."

I recognised the booklet immediately.

"What's wrong?" asked Archer, who was ~~sitting on~~ hugging Reggie to keep him calm. "You look like you might explode."

I shook my head as Mr and Mrs Klaus followed Mum and Dad inside the house. "They've committed one of the biggest Christmas sins," I said, covering my mouth with my hand. "They've . . . They've . . ."

"It's OK, Hols," Archer said gently. "Take your time."

I took a deep breath as Setti and Toby reluctantly stomped towards us. "Archer," I said, swallowing hard. "I think they've regifted your gift."

"So *this* is where you live?" Toby said, snortaughing as he stared at the mishmash of decorations on Dad's workshop. Usually I quite enjoy a snortaugh (snorting while you laugh) or even a snortaughee (snorting so hard while you laugh that you pee!), but coming from Toby, it felt a bit cold and cruel.

I closed the workshop door so Setti and Toby couldn't see inside and led them straight to the back garden.

"I don't know why you're laughing," Archer said, stroking Reggie's ears as he walked with us. "Holly's house is amazing. They have a carol-singing toilet *and* a wrapping room."

"A wrapping *room*?" Setti said. "As in a room to wrap your presents?"

"Yep," I said, trying not to look *too* smug because smugness did not look good on anyone, especially the Klauses, but they had so much smugness they could out-smug a smuggler, who I don't think is actually that smug, so maybe I could be a little bit smug, just this once.

"HA HA HA," Setti roared, laughing so hard I thought she might knock her poinsettia hairband clean off her head. "You think a wrapping room is impressive? *We* have a wrapping *factory*."

"The Klauses' Festive Factory," Toby said.

"A factory so big, it fills the entire basement. A factory so spectacular, it measures the presents, chooses the perfect box size and wraps it all for us."

"Toboggan!" Setti scolded with a wry smile. "There's no need to boast. Holly and Archer have seen our home. They don't need to be reminded how –"

"SET-TI!" Toby yelled. "How many times have I told you not to call me Toboggan?"

Setti stuck her nose in the air and smirked. It was like she actually *enjoyed* making Toby squirm. But after a few moments, when Toby's bottom lip started to quiver, Setti grabbed his hand and squeezed it tight. Toby calmed immediately. Every so often they would smile at each other like they knew something that we didn't. It was weird, but something about their little head nods, secret smiles and side-by-side walking confused me, and it made me feel more uncomfortable than that time I made toilet paper from recycled newspaper and tinsel (ouch!).

NOT SUITABLE

31

I t wasn't long before Setti and Toby were arguing again.

"Take that back!" Toby yelled when Setti told him he was getting shorter.

"You're the worst!" Setti squealed when Toby said she couldn't even spell her own name.

"I'm going to tell Santa!" Toby spat when Setti said she wouldn't share her secret sweet stash.

"You're just –"

"Do you want to see our reindeer?" I interrupted, unable to stand any more of their squabbling.

Setti's competitive grin turned into a furious scowl.

"Reindeer?" she said, wrinkling her nose at Reggie. "Are they all as ugly as that donkey? Because if they are, I think I'll pass."

Toby tried to scoff but choked on his spit. I thought Archer's jaw might hit the ground. And Reggie? Reggie did what he always does when he can't control his emotions.

He tried to fly away.

He ran in circles, leaping into the air and hee-hawing like he was trying to summon all the Christmas magic around us to lift him off the ground and send him galloping into the sky.

"Reggie!" I cried. "You can't fly away right now. We need you here."

Setti and Toby grabbed hold of each other and squealed like piglets.

"Keep your vermin under control!" Toby wailed. "Or at least trade him in for something more suitable."

"*Suitable?*" Archer spluttered.

"It's the word Mother uses when something is less

than perfect," Setti said. "If it's not perfect, then it's not suitable."

"But Reggie *is* perfect!" Archer shouted.

Toby made a *pfft* sound. "What would you lot know about perfection?" he said. "Do you have a hair stylist to do your hair each morning? Have you had etiquette and elocution lessons? Do you travel to Milan each year just to pick a pattern for your Christmas Eve pyjamas?"

"Mee-larn?" I said. "Is that the name of the new charity shop in Lockerton?"

"Charity shop?" Setti screeched. "CHARITY SHOP? Please don't tell me that's where you get your clothes?"

"Of course we do," I said, already feeling slightly more cheerful at the thought of giving unloved clothes a new home.

Setti and Toby looked at each other as if I'd just presented them with a lump of coal.

"Or we make our own clothes from everyday items," I added. "It's called fashionising. You should try it sometime. It's fun and creative and helps spread cheer."

"All I'm hearing right now is blah, blah-blah, blah-blah," Setti said, wiping invisible dust from the arms of her blazer.

I shrank back. Had she sleighriously just said that?

"Do you have to be so mean?" Archer said, comforting both me and Reggie at the same time.

Setti swivelled on her perfectly polished heels. "You're exactly the same, Holly's friend. If you don't have anything intelligent to say then you shouldn't say anything at all."

"CHILDREN!" Mrs Klaus shrieked, clicking her fingers as she flew out of the front door. "It's getting late and you've got a lesson with your sleigh-bell instructor at four."

Setti and Toby trotted to their mum's side without saying goodbye.

"It was a pleasure to see you again, Carrolls," Mr Klaus said with a clenched jaw. "What an . . ." – he stopped to scan the house – ". . . *unusual* home you have." He spread his smile from ear to ear and beamed his blindingly white teeth at us.

"Ta-ta!" Mum shouted, waving her arm above her head like she was conducting an airplane down a runway. "We've had a tinselriffic time. You must come again! For high tea, perhaps? Or supper on the lawn?"

"We could have a dance-off to the festadio!" Dad bellowed, swaying his hips and arms in opposite directions.

"What a winterful idea!" Mum said. "Shall I call you tomorrow? What time do you usually wake? Sunrise? Or earlier?"

"We'll have to get back to you on that," Mrs Klaus said, pulling some oversized sunglasses over her eyes as the Elfler opened the limousine door for them.

"Best not to call us. We'll call you," Mr Klaus agreed, disappearing into the car.

"Mother?" Toby said. "Can we have a –"

"Shhh," Mrs Klaus hissed, pushing him in behind Setti. "Why must you always come to me with questions, Toboggan?" She climbed in after him and slammed the door shut as the Elfler scarpered to the driver's seat and turned on the engine.

"Cheery-ho, Nick!" Mr Klaus called, winding the window down just a crack. "Cheery-ho, Snow. Cheery-ho, kids."

The car jolted forward and reached the end of Sleigh Ride Avenue long before Mum and Dad had stopped waving.

Archer looked at me. "They were making an awfully quick getaway," he said. "Don't you think?"

Ordinarily I would've agreed with Archer, but there was no time to think about the Klauses, or how mean Setti and Toby had been, or the strange reason they left so quickly. Because what happened next was so surprising, it felt like Christmas had come early.

RUN, RUN, RUIN

32

As the Klauses' limo glided out of sight, a tiny black and white shape peered out from behind our snow maze.

"Peep peep!"

"SUUUUE!" Archer and I shouted.

"She escaped the Klauses *again*?" Archer said.

"I suppose there's a lot of room to hide in that limo of theirs," Mum said. "But what in Santa's sleigh is she doing here?"

Sue shivered as she waddled towards me. I scooped her into my arms, noticing her broken flipper had healed, and wrapped her inside my Hollyhood.

"She's cold," I said. "That's why she escaped again. She knows we'll keep her warm."

At the mention of 'keeping warm', Reggie catapulted past us and ran around his stable. "HEE-HAW!" he brayed, motioning at the wooden hut with his head. "HEEEE-HAAAAW!"

Mum and Dad looked at each other, shrugged their shoulders and smiled.

I looked at Archer. "Are you thinking what I'm thinking?" I said, wiggling my eyebrows up and down.

A wide grin spread across Archer's face.

"SLEEPOVER IN THE STABLE!" we shouted.

The rest of the night felt like a dream. I mean, how often do you get to sleep in a stable full of hay, Christmas lights and fluffy blankets with a diva donkey, a dancing penguin and your best friend?

Sue danced around the stable for most of the night. Reggie tried to copy her, but he was as close to becoming a ballerina as he was to flying. I clapped along and sang some Christmas carols, and Archer took photos on the Christmacam.

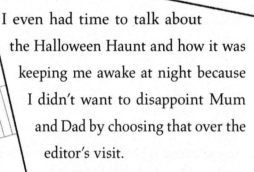

I even had time to talk about the Halloween Haunt and how it was keeping me awake at night because I didn't want to disappoint Mum and Dad by choosing that over the editor's visit.

"You should do what makes you happy," Archer said, munching on some grotto cakes.

"Stop worrying about what your parents want or what Alice and Liena want or even what I want. Do whatever makes *you* happy."

I paused. What *did* make me happy? I'd been so used to spreading cheer to other people that

I had never stopped to think about spreading cheer to myself. I'd always thought that thinking of yourself made you selfish, but if you *never* think of yourself, what does that make you – senseless?

I decided to talk to Dad about the Halloween Haunt in the morning. Surely if I explained how I was feeling, he'd let me go?

When the stars came out and the world fell silent, Sue nuzzled into me, Reggie started snoring, and Archer put the finishing touches to a welcome book he'd made for the editor of *The Christmas Chronicle*. It was the perfect evening, and all thoughts of the Halloween Haunt, the Hallomas party and the Most Festive Family competition sank to the back of my mind.

It wasn't long before the Christmas lights on the house flickered out, and the last thing I remember was Archer letting out the widest yawn I'd ever seen, closing his welcome book and wishing me a Merry Christmas. Then, we fell asleep.

"Holly!" Archer hissed. He was so close to me I could smell his cinnamon breath. "Wake up! Wake up!"

"What's going on?" I mumbled.

"There's someone here," he whispered, the whites of his eyes all huge and panicked. "Actually, I think it might be a few people." He dragged me off my cosy straw bed and pulled me towards the stable door. "LOOK!"

I peered into the moonlit garden. Tall, shadowy figures moved around the house and climbed on to the roof like silent ninjas.

"Do . . . do you think it's Santa?" I said, looking towards the sky for any sign of his reindeer. "Is he practising his Christmas Eve route? Or maybe he sent his elves to help us win the competition?"

Archer put his finger to his lips and ducked down. "I . . . I think it might be burglars, Hols," he whispered.

I yawned. "How can you be thinking about your stomach at a time like this?"

"Not burgers!" Archer said, too terrified to laugh. "Bur-ga-luuurs! As in people trying to steal from you?"

"What?" I gasped. "What should we do? Who should we call?"

"We could call the police?" Archer said. "Or run inside? We could wake your parents?"

"Wait," I said, squinting through the darkness. "I . . . I think they're leaving."

The sound of smashing glass rang through the air, followed by scarpering footsteps and car doors slamming. One by one, three engines rumbled into life and shot down the road. The sound of skidding tyres hung in the air.

"I'm sorry to say it, Hols," Archer said, his voice quiet and quivering. "But I don't think that was Santa."

THE CHRISTMAS BELL 33

The situation grew worse with the sunrise. Our snow cannons, inflatable decorations and life-size sleigh had been broken to pieces and thrown from the roof. Lights lay smashed and in tangled heaps, strewn across the garden. The candy-cane archway that led to the door had been pulled down and thrown on to the road. The snow maze looked like it had been attacked by a monster lawnmower, the refreshmas fountains had been demolished, and some of the fir trees and holly bushes had been pulled clean out of the ground.

"The hobby trees!" Dad wailed, running around

the house in his Christmas cracker pyjamas. "They've destroyed Holly's hobby trees! They've stolen the October wreath from the door. They've spray-painted spiders across the walls. They've chucked pumpkins through our windows!"

"At least we're all safe," Mum said, holding Ivy close and trying not to hyperventilate. "That's the most important thing."

"But the editor will be here in five days. FIVE! How are we supposed to fix everything by then? What are we meant to do?"

Nee-naw nee-naw.

Reggie sleepily poked his head out of the stable door. Sue was balancing on his head, her tiny body fitting perfectly between his pointy ears. "Peep?" she said worriedly.

"Bit early for Halloween shenanigans," a police officer said, stepping out of his car and stretching his back. "What time did you say you heard trespassers?"

At the first sight of the policeman, Sue slid down

Reggie's back and scurried behind the stable door. She was right to hide. We had no idea if the police officer (or Mum and Dad for that matter!) would make us return her to the Klauses. But all I could think about was how much happier she was with us and how badly I wanted to rescue the other penguins, too.

"Oh, officer," Mum said, holding back her tears. "It was around midnight. There arose such a clatter! I sprang from the bed to see what was the matter. Away to the window, I flew like a flash."

The officer raised his eyebrows at Mum. "Why are you reciting *The Night Before Christmas*?" he asked. "Is this all some kind of Halloween prank?"

"NO!" Dad said, sounding appalled. "It's something we do to boost our cheer. Carols. Poems. Christmas songs or greetings. It all helps increase the Christmassiness, wouldn't you agree?"

The police officer smiled broadly, before realising it wasn't a joke and forcing an awkward cough. "Do you have any idea who might have done this?" he said, pulling a notepad and pen from his pocket.

"No!" Dad said. "Who would do such a thing?"

"Bell!" Ivy shouted, trying to wriggle out of Mum's arms. "Christmas bell."

We all turned to where Ivy was pointing.

There, on top of a pile of tangled lights, was a tiny golden bell with a swirly K engraved into it.

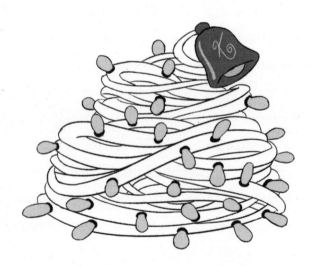

A tiny bell from a stiff blazer collar a certain family was seen wearing yesterday.

"The Klauses must have come back and done this

in the night," said Archer fiercely. "Or hired someone to do it."

"No," Mum said, hiding her mouth behind her hand. "No, they wouldn't have. They're such *lovely* people. They were just coming to check that we were OK after what happened at the Hallomas party. I'm sure they wouldn't have done this."

"Mum," I said. "They weren't checking if we were OK. They came to see if we were a threat."

Mum shook her head – but a few seconds later, her stare hardened. "Are you sure?" she said.

"They wouldn't have done this unless they were scared of losing, Mrs Carroll," Archer said. "So you must have something they don't."

Mum and Dad could barely speak.

"Shall we go inside?" the police officer said, taking off his hat. "I can take a report from the kids before they go to school."

"Shouldn't you arrest the culprits?" Archer said, picking the bell off the ground and handing it to the officer. "They're called Khris and Santalaina Klaus and they live on Candy Cane Lane just over an hour from here. We can come with you. I want to see their faces!"

"I'm afraid it's not as simple as that," the police officer said. "But I admire your gumption, young man. Have you thought about joining the police when you're older?"

Archer huffed loudly as the police officer followed Mum, Dad and Ivy inside. "They can't get away with this!" he said, facing me with ~~stinky~~ steely determination. "Your parents spread more cheer than the Klauses could ever dream of. The Klauses can't just trample over anyone who gets in their way. And they CAN'T win the Most Festive Family competition."

I shrugged hopelessly. "There's not much we can do about it now."

"No, Holly," Archer said, thoughts rolling from his mouth like a snowball growing bigger and bigger and bigger. "The Klauses need to be taught a lesson. If they think it's OK to come here and steal your cheer, let's see how they feel when the tables are turned. Let's see how they feel when they realise they can't always get their own way. Let's see what happens when their penguins are given a proper home, and the editor of *The Christmas Chronicle* finds out how mean they are, and he crowns the Carrolls as the Most Festive Family."

"You really think we can do all of that?" I said, my heart beating fast.

"Ab-snow-lutely!" Archer said. "Let's go."

SNOWSHINE SMILES

34

O K, OK, so we didn't go *right* away. The police officer wanted to ask a few questions, we had to get changed out of our pyjamas, and there was snow way we could leave on an empty stomach, so Dad made us some winterberry waffles while Mum showed the police officer the damage. There was also the little matter of having to go to school, but I didn't let that stand in my way. I spent the whole day thinking about how to show *The Christmas Chronicle* editor how mean the Klauses were, the Halloween Haunt, how to save the penguins, and what to say to Dad when he picked us up.

We waited ~~patiently~~ for the bell to ring at quarter past three, and when Dad picked us up in the Jolly Jeep, we were just about ready with our persuasive speech.

"So you're telling me," Dad said as we drove into Sleigh Ride Avenue ten minutes later, "that you can't help rebuild the hobby trees or replant the holly bushes because you've got some secret plans for the editor of *The Christmas Chronicle* that will blow him away and help us win the competition?"

"That's right," I said.

"And you need to go to Archer's all night to get it done?"

I saw Archer cross his fingers behind his back.

"And you really think that this plan of yours is more important than helping restore all our decorations?" Dad asked.

I squirmed in my seat and covered my face with my Hollyhood. I *really* wasn't good at lying.

Dad sighed. "And you absnowlutely can't tell me what all this is about?"

I looked at Archer for help.

"Holly taught me that the best kind of cheer is surprise cheer," Archer said nervously. "So we, er, thought we'd surprise you, too."

Dad's face burst into a snowshine smile: this special smile where it stretches from ear to ear and almost outshines the snow when sunlight falls on it. It's my absolute favourite and it makes me feel all gooey inside and sometimes I just want to stare at it all day and not do anything else.

"Archer, my boy!" he cried. "After the day we've all had, some surprise cheer is just what we need. Thank you!"

I tried to copy Dad's snowshine smile but I ended up looking like a clown that needed a poo. All I could think about was my churning tummy. It wobbled and gurgled and felt full and empty all at the same time. Was this what guilt felt like? All this lying and tricking and sneaking around?

I was desperate to ask Dad about the Halloween Haunt again, but after the house got ruined and his cheer-o-meter rating went from a ten to a two, the idea of his Christmas-obsessed child going to a Halloween party might just push him over the edge.

"Archer," I whispered queasily. "I really don't like lying to Dad."

"It's not lying," Archer whispered back. "We're going to tell him eventually. It's just . . . withholding the truth for a while. Like giving someone a present and letting them open it when they're ready."

The corners of my mouth rose. Archer had such a talent for putting my mind at ease.

"Let's help clear up for a bit," I said quietly as Dad pulled up outside the house. "Before we go to Candy Cane Lane. There will be loads of people helping. I bet it won't take long."

As I stepped out of the car, a few people walked past me carrying wrenches, paintbrushes and buckets of soap. *Very* few. Five, in fact.

Oh.

"I thought the whole neighbourhood would be here," I said. "Doesn't everyone in Lockerton support the way we celebrate Christmas all year?"

"They do, Snowflake," Dad sighed. "But everyone has their own jobs and busy lives. They can't just drop everything to help us win a competition. Besides, most of the decorations were hand-made. One-offs. Inventions I spent years creating. We're not going to get those back any time soon, but I'm very grateful for Eddie, Rishi, Esme, Prisha and Norman. They've been very kind to give up some of their time."

Dad tried to look cheerful as he pointed everyone out. But he looked *so* disappointed. He was one of those people that would do anything to help anyone. Even if that meant giving them clothes off his own back, or spending an entire week helping them fix their car or repaint their house. I so badly wanted to help him.

"Refreshments!" Mum called, walking out of the house with a tray of snowiches. She placed them on the bonnet of the Jolly Jeep and waved the volunteers over. "Thank you, Eddie," she said, adding some tinsel to Eddie's tool belt and a Santa hat on his bald head. "We didn't think we'd find a plumber at such short notice. Thank you, Rishi and Esme, for offering to replant the trees, and Prisha, for your excellent painting skills. And to you, Norman, for being the most snowtacular handyman we could wish for!"

Norman blushed and pushed his round glasses up the bridge of his nose. "Don't mention it," he said, his bushy moustache jiggling like a fuzzy caterpillar. "I'm no expert, but I'll do what I can."

"Don't you need to be getting back to your kids soon?" Mum said, whipping a flask of hot chocolate from her apron pocket and offering a cup to Norman. "How many did you say you had again? Would they like to come and visit the reindeer sometime?"

Norman smiled and walked around the garden talking to Mum about his children, our love for Christmas, and the different things he would help us fix by the end of the week.

This was what Mum and Dad did best. They knew how to speak to people. They knew how to be kind and show empathy and listen to people's stories. And when their whole world came crashing down around them, they knew how to spread cheer, even when they didn't feel it themselves.

All the feelings of guilt and tension and helplessness hardened in my stomach. I knew I shouldn't be planning to sneak off to Candy Cane Lane again, but I couldn't just sit around and let someone wreck our house, ruin Dad's decorventions, and destroy Mum's dream of becoming the Most Festive Family.

"Come on, Archer," I said, offering him the last snowich from the tray. "We can't let the Klauses get away with this."

Archer split the snowich in two and gave me the bigger half. "You sure you want to go?" he said, swinging his backpack on to his shoulder. "Now?"

I nodded. "Now."

We hadn't even made it to the end of the garden when Reggie and Sue came running after us.

"Hee-haw," Reggie brayed, hopping from hoof to hoof.

"Peep peep," Sue cried, balancing herself between Reggie's ears.

"Of course you two want to come with us!" I laughed. "Are you sure you're up to the challenge?"

Reggie nodded. Sue gave a salute with her flipper.

"I guess we could use as much help as we can get," Archer said, smiling as Reggie peered from left to right like a secret ~~investigator~~ inreindeergator. "But you won't go running off this time, will you, Reggie?"

Reggie grinned and nuzzled into Archer.

"OK, then," I said. "Operation Spread Cheer, Not Fear is on! Let's go . . ."

HOLLY
JOLLY
GOLLY

35

I n theory, the plan was simple. The Klauses might be happy to spread fear by destroying our house in the middle of the night, but we were all about spreading CHEER. We wanted to spread cheer to the penguins by finding them a happy new home in a local zoo. We wanted to spread cheer to Mum and Dad by helping them win the Most Festive Family competition. We even wanted to spread cheer to the Klauses themselves by showing them the real meaning of Christmas. Sure, losing their dancing penguins wouldn't make their home any less christmariffic or their faces any less sour, but they might just realise how un-Christmassy and hurtful they'd been.

If nothing else, we hoped the editor of *The Christmas Chronicle* would find out about the Klauses' mean behaviour. They called Sue a 'Nuisance', they kept dancing penguins for their own amusement, and they wrecked our house and all of Dad's decorventions in an effort to wipe us out of the competition! Surely the editor would *never* call them the Most Festive Family once he found that out? Archer had an idea to write him an anon-ee-mouse email, but I secretly hoped the Klauses would pull out of the competition themselves. I know it was wishful thinking, but I believed in magic and wishes more than I believed in gravity, and when it came to Christmas, *anything* was possible.

"Right," I said, my insides squirming as Archer, Reggie, Sue and I hopped off the bus and walked towards Candy Cane Lane. "So I'll tell the security elf-ficer that I'm here to see Setti and Toby. He knows me, so he'll let me in without too many questions . . . hopefully."

Archer nervously shoved his hands in his pockets.

"And while you distract him, I'll unplug the screens in his office so he won't see us sneak into the Ice Quarter,' he said. 'I'll pop some clear sticky tape over the ends of the plugs so that when he tries to put them back in, they won't work. Hopefully he won't realise what we've done until we're gone."

"And once you've . . ." I paused.

Why could I barely see the Candy Cane Lane sign? Why weren't the trees lit up? Why could I only see a shadowy outline of the elf-ficer in his dark booth? I pulled Archer, Reggie and Sue behind a parked car on the opposite side of the road.

"What's wrong?" Archer said, looking to the sky as if a giant spotlight would fall on us at any moment.

"The lights are out," I said. "All of them. Something

strange is going on. And . . ." I squinted into the distance. "Does the guard look different to you? He looks taller. Slimmer?"

"Oh no!" Archer gasped. "It's a new security officer! How are we going to get past him now?"

"Affirmative, Mr Klaus," the new elf-ficer said into his mobile phone. "The lights are off in my cabin, too. I would've noticed earlier but I was having my induction." He paused, wiped his brow and then raised the phone to his ear again. "The other guy was meant to man the cabin until the end of the day. Bit of a mystery where he went. I'll write everything in the log book and see what I can do about getting the cameras back on."

Archer threw his arms in the air. "What are we going to do now? This new security guard isn't just going to

let us in. He'll call Mr and Mrs Klaus. Or check if we're on the guest list – which we're not, by the way!"

As Sue let out a nervous 'peep', Reggie jumped on us with a *splat* and forced us flat on the ground.

"Good plan," Archer said, his breathing fast and erratic. "Hide and stay quiet. Camp out here till the coast is clear. Lie low until –"

"HOLLY JOLLY GOLLY!" I yelled, making Archer jump a metre in the air. "HOLLY JOLLY GOLLY! HOLLY JOLLY GOLLY!"

"What are you *doing*?" Archer gasped, grabbing at my jumper to pull me back down. "Have you totally lost your mind?"

The new security elf-ficer shot out of his seat as if someone had lit fireworks under his chair. As he grabbed his hat off a hook on the wall, he dropped his coffee mug with a loud *SMASH* and almost fell out of the security hut. Then he sprinted through the dark fir-tree forest and out of sight.

Archer watched, wide-eyed. "Did you put him under

some magical Christmas spell? Why did he run away like that?"

"It's the secret password," I said. "Remember? It's what you have to shout if you get lost. Or if there's a fire. I can't remember which one exactly. But it worked, didn't it? He's gone."

"Holly!" Archer breathed. "You're a genius."

"Come on," I whispered, tucking Sue under my arm as Reggie stealthily slid his belly along the ground. "This might be our only chance to get inside."

KREEPY KLAUSES

We crept down the long, narrow driveway in darkness, clinging on to each other and whispering as quietly as we dared. The shadows of the trees reflected on the mirrored ground and made them look like creepy swamp monsters trying to reach out and grab us. I didn't understand. Did the Klauses know we were coming? Were they trying to scare us? Had they completely changed their minds about the Most Festive Family competition and now they wanted to become the Kreepy Klauses instead?

"I don't like this, Arch," I said. "Something feels . . . off."

As fear rose in my chest, my heart yearned for the taste of cinnamon and hot chocolate. It longed for the feel of a cosy blanket and a warm hug, or a comforting Christmas card from a friend. I hummed the first two verses of *We Wish You A Merry Christmas* to calm my nerves, but it was no good. As we reached the end of the deserted driveway, the ground beneath our feet began to sink and squelch, and any ounce of Christmas cheer vanished in an instant.

"The icy ground!" Archer gasped, holding his arms out like he was caught in quicksand. "It's melting!"

"So are the snow fountains," I said, pointing at the misshapen piles of snow collapsing in the moonlight.

"Hee-haaaaw!" Reggie cried, his whole body shaking.

Archer took Sue from me and nestled her between Reggie's ears. "Even the house lights are off!" he said as Sue and Reggie nuzzled close. "Do you think the Klauses are on holiday? Or trying to save money on the electricity bill?"

Suddenly, a whirring siren filled the air.

"STOP RIGHT THERE!" an angry voice yelled.

The security elf-ficer and three guards sprang from the woods. Reggie let out a startled yelp and darted off in the other direction with Sue clinging to his inflatable antlers. It was stupid of us to think he wouldn't run off. He was such a scaredy-~~cat~~ ~~donkey~~ reindeer. To be honest, if I could have run as fast as him, I probably would've scarpered, too.

As the guards closed in on me and Archer with terrifying scowls, a long, sleek car pulled up to the house, its beaming headlights shining in our eyes. The car slowed and the windows wound down.

Mr and Mrs Klaus glared at us with such venom, I was surprised lasers didn't shoot out of their eyes.

"What is going on here?" Mrs Klaus demanded. "You called us about a power cut but this is a complete power *failure*!"

"The damage is vast, ma'am," the security elf-ficer explained. "The Ice Quarter has completely melted, the penguins have fled, the Toy Quarter has flooded and the fridges in the Village Quarter have been off for hours, so all the award-winning food is inedible." He pointed at me and Archer. "These two children have really made a mess of things."

"What?" I gasped. "We didn't do any of this!"

Setti, Toby and the Elfler appeared at the front door. They were wearing red satin pyjamas and held huge silver lanterns with candles inside. It was hard to see them through the shadows, but I was sure I saw Toby's lip quivering and Setti shivering from the cold. How long had they been without heating and electricity?

"We're sorry to wake you, children," the new elf-ficer yelled, stiffening his square shoulders. "Go back inside. Stay warm. We've got this under control."

Setti and Toby disappeared inside as Mr and Mrs Klaus opened the doors of their dark green limousine and stepped out. They were dressed in gold velvet coats and fur-trimmed scarves and had at least one hundred shopping bags piled high on the seats behind them.

"*Sabotage!*" Mr Klaus spat, staring at us with piercing

green eyes. "Coming on to our private land. Ruining Klausland. Doing thousands of pounds' worth of damage! Who do you think you are?"

Mrs Klaus placed her hand on his shoulder and he stopped talking immediately.

"Take them inside," she said, her voice calm and cold. "I've called the police."

STAMPING OUT THE COMPETITION

37

"We knew your cheery dispositions were just a visard," Mr Klaus hissed. With lanterns in both hands, he escorted us through their giant entrance hall and along a wide corridor lined with oil paintings of themselves posing with Father Christmas.

"A vis-what?" I said, my heart thumping like reindeer hooves on a roof.

"A vis*aaaard*," Mr Klaus repeated. "A mask. An act. A fake pretence to make us like you. Nobody is that cheerful all the time."

"Father Christmas is," I said.

Mr Klaus sniffed. "Yes, well, *you're* not Father Christmas, little girl," he said. "And you'll never be as cheery as he is after today. You'll be going straight to the top of the naughty list. A lump of coal in your stocking will be too kind, if you ask me."

"But you wrecked the Carrolls' house!" Archer fought back. "So you'll be on the naughty list, too."

"I assure you, dear boy," Mrs Klaus interrupted, smoothing a few flyaway hairs from her giant bauble-shaped hairstyle. "*We* did nothing of the sort."

There was something about the way she said 'we' . . .

"You mean, you *paid* someone to wreck the Carrolls' house for you?" Archer gasped. "You can't even do your own dirty work?"

Mr Klaus licked his oversized teeth and ran his fingers through his slicked-back hair. "When you have money, dear boy, you can pay people to do anything."

"Like Klausland," Mrs Klaus added, spreading her arms wide. "We'll have this place fixed before you can say 'credit card'. In fact, I think we should go back to Harrods first thing in the morning, don't you, darling? Eugene, make an appointment with our personal shoppers."

Wow, they weren't even denying it.

"You're wrong!" I yelled, standing as tall as I could – which, compared to the Klauses, wasn't that tall, but

I was definitely taller than I'd been last week, so I was taking that as a win. "Money can't buy manners or kindness or compassion."

"And what makes you think we need those?" Mrs Klaus said, her tinkleless-bell laugh making the hairs on my neck stand on end. "Like my darling husband said, when you have money, you get what you want without the need for niceties."

"But what about spreading cheer?" I cried. "And putting others before yourself? And finding happiness in the small things?"

Mrs Klaus raised her hand. "All I'm hearing right now is blah, blah-blah, blah-blah."

My brain jumped back to Setti and Toby in our garden. Wasn't that exactly what Setti had said?

As if picturing them inside my head had made them magically appear in front of me, Setti and Toby poked their heads around the corner of the corridor and ran towards us.

"Mother! Father!" they called. "We've been in

darkness all day. We've been so scared!"

"Did I give you permission to speak?" Mrs Klaus snapped, squeezing the bridge of her nose with the tips of her fingers. "Please get out of my sight, children. It's been a very stressful shopping day, and unless I have a glass of festive fizz in my hand, I don't think I can handle looking at your grubby faces a moment longer."

Toby licked his palm and rubbed his cheek until it turned red. Setti wiped a tear from her eye and then grabbed Toby's hand and stormed away.

"Now," Mrs Klaus said, clicking her fingers for the Elfler. "It's time to stamp out the competition once and for all. What is your parents' phone number, little girl? They need to be here when the police arrive."

As the Elfler escorted us to the Tree and Treat Room, Archer and I caught glimpses of Klausland through the long corridor windows.

"Whoa!" I whispered, nudging Archer so we could hang back from the Elfler. "Klausland really is ruined."

Temporary floodlights lit up the ski mountain, and

we could just make out the melting Ice Quarter with its ice statues and ice bridges and enormous ice rink turning to puddles in front of our eyes.

"Who could have done it?" Archer said, slipping closer to the window to get a better look. "The Klauses must've been using really cold air conditioning, or giant freezers or underground pipes that pump out cold air to stop everything from thawing. It would have taken a lot of effort to ruin *everything*!"

"It's not just who could have done it, Archie, but WHY?"

"My bet is the Elfler," Archer said quietly. "Or the original security guard who mysteriously left. It's got to be someone close to the Klauses. Someone with access to the house and the security systems. Someone the Klauses upset or offended."

The Elfler clicked his fingers and we scurried into the Trick or Treat Room where a few lanterns had been lit in the corners of the room.

Without so much as a 'goodbye', 'so long' or a tippetytap of his curly elf shoe, the Elfler slammed the door shut and turned the key.

"This isn't good, Hols," Archer said, nervously biting his nails. "We only came to do something good. To –"

"Shhh!" I said, putting my finger to my mouth. "Can you hear that?"

Archer strained his ear and widened his eyes.

"Someone's here."

THE CHEERLESS CHILDREN

38

Archer and I tiptoed around the room like silent nelfjas. We hid behind towering Christmas trees and giant velvet curtains, and did over-the-top hand gestures that made us feel like super spies. It wasn't until we reached the centre of the room and hid ourselves in the branches of a tree that we remembered we weren't supposed to be having fun and that there was poo-ten-telly someone else in the room with us.

"I told you, Toby!" a quiet voice hissed. "They have no idea it was us. Mother and Father think it was Holly and Archer and that's the story we're sticking to, OK?"

My heart dropped.

"But what if they *do* realise it was us?" Toby's voice whispered. "We shouldn't have done it, Setti. We're going to be in so much trouble. What if we don't get any presents ever again?"

Slowly, Archer and I peered around the corner of the tree. Setti and Toby were huddled on the floor, half hidden under the low-lying branches and stacks of presents.

"Hi," I said, making them jump. "I think we need to talk. Don't you?"

We sat down beside Setti and Toby and waited for them to speak. The light from their lanterns flickered across the room and glinted off the crystal baubles on the Christmas trees. It actually felt a little magical, cosy . . . almost *nice*. But Setti and Toby were squirming awkwardly and could barely look us in the eye.

"Can I ask you a question?" I said, my voice echoing around the room.

"If you must," Setti muttered.

"Do your parents always speak to you like that?"

"Like what?" Toby said.

"You know," I replied. "Do they always send you away? Do they tell you to stop talking, or say 'blah, blah, blah' at you all the time?"

"Not *always*," Setti said. "Just when we catch them at the wrong time. Or when they've had a less than perfect day."

"Or when they've got guests," Toby added. "But we get extra presents when guests come over, so it's not all bad."

I nodded like I understood what they were saying. But the truth was, I didn't. Mum and Dad never sent me away if I wanted to talk to them. And when we had guests over, we worked together to make them feel as welcome as possible. We gave them snowshine smiles and food and cheer, and we never expected presents in return.

"This competition has brought out the worst side of Mother and Father," Setti said quietly. "We've never seen them like this. They're used to getting whatever they want, and when they get what they want, they're happy."

Toby nodded. "And if *they're* happy, *we're* happy. But lately . . ."

"Lately they've been worried," Setti said, holding Toby's hand to comfort him. "We've done everything we can to be perfect children, but all they can think about is the Most Festive Family competition. You're really making them sweat."

"We're making THEM sweat?" I laughed, lightening the mood. "Have you SEEN your house? You've got a theme park, a ski mountain and an entire Christmas village in your back garden. What more could you want?"

"Dad said something about the 'homely' touch," Setti explained. "He thought we could learn a thing or two from your family about how to make a house feel cosy for Christmas. That's the real reason we visited you."

"Father was on the phone to his interior designer the whole way home," Toby added.

"Great," I said, rolling my eyes. "So not only do you have all of this, but now you're going to make your house feel warm and welcoming, too?"

"Mother and Father don't stop until they reach perfection," Toby said. "It's a bit exhausting, if I'm honest."

"We know how lucky we are," Setti said, flattening Toby's flyaway hair and straightening his posture. "We get everything we ask for and more. Mother and Father give us the perfect life in the perfect home with perfect memories. But I didn't realise until we came to your house just how much we were missing."

My mouth hung open. "But you just said you have everything you want!"

Toby and Setti looked at each other nervously. For the first time I noticed how much they relied on each other. I noticed how Setti took care of Toby and Toby agreed with every little thing Setti said. They were more than siblings. They were each other's support system. They were partners in crime. They were best friends.

"What I really want is to decorate a tree myself," Setti said at last. "I want Mum to put one of my hand-made ornaments on the fireplace instead of the expensive crystal ones she gets from Harrods. I want to use the ski slope whenever I want, not just the day before the fresh snow arrives."

"And I want to make a gingerbread house," Toby chipped in. "With sloppy icing and extra jelly sweets and a wonky roof. I want to eat it as soon as it's finished, or at least take chunks out of it when no one is looking."

"We've never sung carols together," Setti said sadly.

"Mother said I was out of tune and needed more lessons. And we can't even wrap our own presents because the stupid Festive Factory does it for us."

"You have all of that," Toby mumbled. "You make cool inventions and you bake together in the kitchen. Your mum teaches you how to sew and you have friends that write you Christmas carols. That's what our house is missing. And that's why we won't win the competition. That's why we *shouldn't* win the competition."

I was so shocked you'd think Toby and Setti had randomly sprouted reindeer antlers.

"So is that why you wrecked your own house?" I said. "For *us*?"

"Don't flatter yourself," Setti said, pulling her poinsettias out of her hair. "We still *want* to win. But, ummm . . ."

"It's OK," Archer said. "You can tell us. We won't say a word."

Setti lifted her chin. "We did it for us," she said. "To show Mother and Father that there's more important things to Christmas than pretending to be perfect."

"You mean, you did it for attention?" I said.

Setti gulped. "OK, maybe that's more accurate." She gazed at Toby who was staring at his velvet slippers. He looked like he wanted to say something but kept changing his mind. He opened and closed his mouth a few times but only a squeak came out. It was only when Setti squeezed his hand that he took a deep breath and looked me square in the eye.

"We just want them to love us as much as they love Christmas," he said.

A FESTIVE FRIENDSHIP 39

"You took your time, officer!" Mrs Klaus's voice shrilled down the corridor an hour or two later. "You should see the damage they've caused. They deserve to be disqualified from the Most Festive Family competition at the very least!"

Setti stiffened. Toby closed his eyes.

"What are we going to do?" Archer hissed at me.

I shrugged my shoulders. If only I had Santa's direct line! I bet I could call him and he'd arrive in his sleigh in the blink of an eye to save us.

But help came from someone else.

Someone surprising.

"Go," Toby said, pointing at the open window. "We'll say we haven't seen you."

"Yes," Setti said, pushing us towards the window. "Go. Quickly!"

My eyes widened. Were Setti and Toby being *selfless*?

"Actually," I said, checking the door was still shut. "I think you two should go. Your parents don't need to know you had anything to do with this."

"You're going to take the blame?" Setti said, like she didn't believe what she was hearing.

"You don't need another reason for your parents to be upset with you," agreed Archer. "I know they can probably pay to get everything fixed by tomorrow, but why don't you offer to do it instead? Show them you can fix Klausland as a family?"

Setti's mouth opened and closed like a fish. "We've never . . . No one has ever . . ."

The door to the Tree or Treat Room banged open.

"THERE!" Mrs Klaus shouted, pointing at us just as the electricity came back on and the giant Christmas tree chandeliers sprang into life. "That's who you need to arrest, officer!"

The sound of Dad's squeaky reindeer trainers echoed in the distance, followed by Mum's favourite sleigh-bell skirt that had so many layers, it sounded like a ten-piece orchestra.

"What in Santa's beard is going on?" Dad yelled. I could hear the panic and worry and love in his voice and I wanted nothing more than to run into his arms and stay there forever.

"Ah, Carrolls," Mr Klaus sneered as Mum, Dad and Ivy raced into the room with the Elfler at their heels. "You're just in time to hear your daughter, er . . ." He clicked his fingers at me.

"Holly," Setti said, chucking her poinsettia across the floor. "Her name is HOLLY."

My heart filled with ~~pride~~ ~~gratitude~~ ~~Christmas cheer~~ ALL the feelings. I mouthed 'thank you', unable to wipe the snowshine smile off my face.

"Yes, yes, that's the one," Mr Klaus said. "You're

just in time to see Holly and her friend confess to the abominable crime they've committed."

"'It wasn't them, Father," Toby whispered as more police officers entered the room.

"We haven't invited you to speak, Toboggan," Mrs Klaus snapped. "Come here. Both of you."

But Setti and Toby stayed where they were. Setti even edged a little closer and reached for my hand.

"I'm sure this is just some terrible misunderstanding," Mum said, trying her best to keep calm and composed, which we all knew was NOT one of her biggest strengths. I noticed her 'Sleigh Whaaaat?' T-shirt was on back to front and her mascara was smudged around her eyes.

"It is," I said. "I'm sorry, Mum. I didn't meant to upset you."

Mum's bottom lip quivered. A wave of guilt and ~~worry exhaustion~~

worhaustion washed over me.

"We were just trying to help," I said, words tumbling from my mouth before I could stop them. "We were going to rescue all the penguins. We thought it would solve everything. We thought it would give them a happy new home where they wouldn't be forced to dance all day, and we thought it would show the Klauses that how they've been treating the penguins – and us – is wrong."

"Holly's right," Archer said. "We thought we could show the Klauses how unhappy Sue and the penguins were and that maybe they'd realise the true meaning of Christmas. I was even going to tell the editor of *The Christmas Chronicle* so that he knew all the facts before he decided who would win the competition."

"We were doing it all to spread cheer," I said. "Or, at least, we were trying to, but –"

"Excuse me?" one of the police officers said. "Did you say penguins? As in, *real* penguins?"

I nodded my head so hard I almost gave myself whiplash. "The Klauses are keeping penguins here and they're making them dance and —"

"Hang on, Hols," Archer said, turning his head towards the open window. "Do you hear that?"

Normally I hated having my epic non-stop speeches disturbed, but Archer was right. There was a strange noise. It was *very* faint. But the sound was unmistakable.

"Eeeeeawwwww . . ." The strange sound travelled on the breeze and gradually grew clearer. "Eee-aaaaw. Eee-haaaw. Heeeee-haaaaw."

"Wait," I said. "Is that . . ."

I joined Archer at the window. He pointed at the top of the Klausland ski mountain and widened his eyes.

"There," he said. "On the toboggan track."

A grey, fuzzy blur twisted around the mountainside. It whizzed and whirled and whooshed so quickly, I thought the toboggan might fly off the rails all together, but somehow, the grey ball of fuzz managed to stay upright. It zoomed closer to the Trick or Treat Room, and I realised what — or should I say who — it was.

"Weggie!" Ivy squealed. "Weggie's coming!"

FLYING FREE

40

I blinked once. Twice. Three times.

The sound drained from the world.

Was this how Father Christmas felt on Christmas Eve?

Was my beloved, smelly, attention-seeking, scaredy-donkey-reindeer best friend about to . . .

"Quick!" Archer yelled. "Grab the curtains!"

Mr and Mrs Klaus were rooted to the spot, but Mum, Dad, Setti, Toby, Archer, the Elfler and even a few of the police officers ran around the room and tore down the thick velvet curtains that hung across the floor-to-ceiling windows. There were at least ten windows, so by the time the curtains had been piled high in front of the open window, we had created the perfect landing pad.

Landing pad? I hear you ask. Why would we need a landing pad?

Get ready for a Christmas miracle, everyone . . .

Reggie had finally learned to fly.

"Reggie!" I yelled, clapping my hands so hard they hurt. "You're doing it, you're doing it!"

Reggie launched himself off the end of the toboggan track and flew through the air with his inflatable antlers blowing behind him and his slobbery tongue wagging in the wind. For a moment he looked like a real reindeer, his legs running on air and his head proudly pointing towards the sky.

"Go, Reggie!" Archer yelled, jumping up and down at the window.

Timing it perfectly, Reggie flew through the open window of the Tree or Treat Room at just the right angle and landed on the pile of curtains with a triumphant 'HEEEEE-HAAAAAW!'

Archer and I gave him a round of applause. Reggie

wiggled off the giant curtain pile and sprinted to my side. Then, before I could so much as hug him or get a whiff of his excited farts (which I just realised we should probably call exifarts), some high-pitched peeping filled the air.

"Stand back," Dad shouted. "I think Reggie's brought company."

"NO!" Mrs Klaus shouted. "Those creatures will NOT be coming inside. Absolutely not. I forbid it. They're vermin. They're rodents. They're –"

"PENGUIIIINS!" Ivy squealed, clapping her hands with excitement.

One by one, the dancing penguins appeared on the last few metres of the toboggan run. When they'd gained enough speed, they leaped into the air, aimed directly for the Tree or Treat Room, and elegantly twirled through the open window. As each one plopped on to the pile of curtains, Mrs Klaus let out a whimper.

"They're inside the house, Khris!" she wailed.

"I can see that, Laina," Mr Klaus barked, his neck turning as red and pimply as a sunburnt toad. "But at least that *nuisance* isn't here. That one would go crashing into every Christmas tree and bring down the chandeliers if it could!"

"Actually, Mr Klaus," Archer said. "I think you'll find she's a pretty spectacular penguin. And she's about to make the biggest entrance of them all."

While Mr and Mrs Klaus turned the colour of Reggie's pale grey bum, the rest of us ran to the windows to give Sue the audience she deserved.

The little penguin was waiting like a perfectly poised ballerina at the very top of the mountain. She looked evey tinier from down here. As we watched, she waddled forward and slipped down the toboggan run on the tip of her oversized foot. With her other foot extended behind her and her flippers fanned out wide, she turned her head to the sky like all the stars were watching.

It was undubidedly one of the most beautiful and graceful things I had ever seen.

As Sue soared off the end of the toboggan run and flew towards us, she held her position, her neck extended to the side, her flippers framing her curved tummy and her oversized foot displayed proudly behind her for everyone to see. She pirouetted through the window and landed on the curtain pile with a neat curtsey.

The applause was so loud it drowned out Reggie's exifarts. One of the police officers even pulled out his phone to take a photo.

"That was incredible!" I said, running to Sue's side as the other penguins wobbled around her and gathered for a big group hug. "You're the most beautiful dancer I've ever seen, Sue."

"Hee-haw!" Reggie agreed, his head bouncing up and down.

"That . . . that was amazing!" Setti gasped.

"I've never seen anything like it," Archer agreed.

Toby crouched down in front of Sue. "Could we join your group hug?" he said.

Sue let out a little 'peep' and that was how we ended up in a penguin, human, ~~donkey~~ reindeer embrace until Mr and Mrs Klaus found their voices again.

"This . . ." Mr Klaus said, the red pimples now rising to his cheeks and nose, "this is an OUTRAGE. You come into our home. You wreck our decorations. You let your pet loose in Klausland. You try to steal our penguins. You –"

"So you admit they're your penguins?" a police officer said, raising one eyebrow impressively high.

"Well, er, I," Mr Klaus fumbled.

"Have you read the Animal Welfare Act?" another officer said.

"We don't need to!" Mrs Klaus insisted. "We paid a huge sum for those penguins and have had the very best trainers money can buy, to teach them how to dance. They belong to us."

"They *belong* in the wild," the first police officer said. "Or at least in a registered zoo where they can be properly cared for."

"Hang on," Mr Klaus said. "You aren't here to talk about the penguins. You're here to talk about how the Carrolls have tried to sabotage our glorious home and cheat us out of winning the Most Festive Family competition."

The officers looked at each other and shook their heads.

"There are more urgent matters to attend to right now, Mr Klaus," one of them said, pulling out his notebook and pen. "How long exactly have you had these penguins?"

"What species of penguin are they?" another officer asked. "And who sold them to you?"

"I . . . I . . . I . . ." Mr Klaus spluttered.

The police officer with the high-raised eyebrows turned to face us. "We checked the security footage, Mr and Mrs Carroll. Holly and Archer arrived five minutes before Mr and Mrs Klaus got home. They could never have caused this much chaos in that time. You are all free to go."

TIME TO TALK

41

"FREE TO GO?"

Mrs Klaus's voice was so ear-splittingly loud, I was surprised the windows didn't shatter.

"That's right," the police officer said. "In fact, I'm sure it was nothing more than a power cut. And with all of these electrics you've got hooked up, I'm surprised it hasn't happened sooner."

Mrs Klaus looked so outraged, I thought her head might pop off.

"Actually, Mum," Setti said. "It wasn't just a power cut."

Toby grabbed Setti's hand. "Yeah. We, er, have

something to tell you."

The whole room fell silent as Setti gathered the courage to explain.

"We were upset when you went shopping without us . . . again."

"You didn't even have breakfast with us or say goodbye," Toby said.

"And when we found the new electrics room while we were playing hide-and-seek, we sort of fell on to some switches and turned the power off by accident."

"We didn't *mean* to," Toby agreed. "But we didn't rush to turn them back on either."

Setti repeated everything she'd told us earlier about wanting to decorate the trees and sing carols and wrap presents themselves, and how what she really wanted for Christmas was to spend time as a family.

By the end of their confession, Mr Klaus looked like he'd fallen down a chimney and didn't know how to get back out. His beaming smile had lost its sparkle, his shoulders had sagged, and a few wrinkles had etched their way across his tight forehead. Even Mrs Klaus looked like a piece of crumpled wrapping paper. She was still beautiful and bright, but she was also worn and tired, and everything about her looked a little less . . . perfect.

"I'm sorry to interrupt," the police officer said, tapping his watch. "The Animal Crime Unit will arrive soon and we still need to take your statements. Is there somewhere quiet we can go to ask some questions?"

Mr Klaus ran his tongue over his teeth. "Yes," he said after a moment. "We can use my office."

"Mother, Father," Setti said, her bottom lip quivering. "Is there anything we can do?"

Mrs Klaus gazed at Setti with watery eyes. Mr Klaus reached into his pocket for his comb, but changed his mind and crouched down in front of Setti and Toby instead.

"We tried to give you everything you ever wanted," he said. "But you're telling us that it's not enough?"

"It's not that it's not enough," Toby said. "I actually

think you've given us *too* much."

"We have so many toys and clothes and hobbies that there's no time for anything else," Setti agreed. "There's no *family* time."

Mrs Klaus covered her mouth. "I . . . I'm sorry, Poinsettia. We had no idea. I was just spoiling you the way I wanted to be spoilt as a child. I thought it would make you happy."

"I think Setti and Toby love being spoilt with presents," I said, not wanting the Klauses' heart-to-heart to end. "But I think they want to be spoilt with your *presence* more."

Mr and Mrs Klaus stared at me with wide, unblinking eyes.

"Is that true?" Mrs Klaus whispered.

Setti and Toby nodded.

"Well then," Mrs Klaus said, patting her bauble-styled hair to compose herself. "I suppose that means you'll be coming shopping with us tomorrow to pick out new decorations for Klausland."

Toby blinked. "We will?"

"And we'll have to go for lunch while the decoration team rebuild the snow fountains," added Mr Klaus.

"Can we have hot chocolate and mince pies when we get back?" Setti said. "And maybe watch a Christmas movie together?"

"Only if we wrap presents for the editor of *The Christmas Chronicle* at the same time," Mrs Klaus said.

I thought Setti's jaw might actually hit the floor. "Toby and I are allowed to wrap presents?"

"I think the editor will quite like the home-made touch," Mrs Klaus said.

"And what about you, Mother? What would YOU would like?" Setti asked cautiously.

Mrs Klaus let out a long, deep sigh.

"Actually, Poinsettia," she said. "I think I'd like a hug."

Setti and Toby ran forward and wrapped their arms around their parents like they'd been away for years and years and had finally been reunited. Mrs Klaus held Toby tighter than Santa gripped the reins on

Christmas Eve. And Mr Klaus whispered something so funny into Setti's ear, she burst into a fit of giggles and couldn't stop.

"You know what, Hols?" Archer said as the Klauses hugged and the police officers rounded up the penguins. "I don't think the Klauses are bad people. I just think they're used to getting everything they ever wanted.

But tonight has made them realise there's one thing they don't have."

"Our carol-singing toilet seat?" I said.

Archer laughed. "No. Gratitude. They were always so focused on getting the next big thing. The next diamond-encrusted decoration. The next award-winning meal. The next celebrity guest. They were always looking for cheer in the things they could buy, but they were never grateful for any of it."

"Isn't there a saying?" I said. "About money not buying happiness?"

"Exactly!" said Archer.

My heart tingled as Setti slipped her hand inside her dad's and they walked off, their arms swinging.

"The greatest cheer doesn't come from expensive clothes or fancy things," I said. "It comes from people. And laughter. And making memories."

"And being grateful for what you already have," Archer agreed.

A warm, fuzzy feeling settled in my chest. Maybe

everything was about to change for the Klauses. Maybe they'd finally learned what was really important.

"Mother?" Toby said. "Did you get me a present from your shopping trip?"

"Now, Toboggan, we talked about this . . ."

"But Muuuum . . ."

OK. Maybe not *everything* would change. But it was a start.

PROUD PARENT

42

I spent the whole journey home making a giant 'Reggie is my hero' badge. Somehow, he'd ~~single-handedly~~ single-hoofedly rescued Sue and the other penguins, taught Mr and Mrs Klaus a lesson, and helped bring Setti and Toby closer to their parents. AND, on top of all that, he'd actually *flown*. Like a real reindeer. I thought my heart might burst like a present that was wrapped too tightly.

But it didn't last long. I might have felt like a proud parent, but apparently Mum and Dad did *not*. Dad could barely look at me and Mum's uncontrollable whimpers made the air in my lungs wobble.

"You lied to us, Holly," Dad said sternly, driving without the festadio on for the first time ever. "You said you were going to Archer's house. You said you had a surprise for the editor that would help us win the competition."

"We did have a surprise for him!" I said. "We were going to show him how unhappy the penguins were. We were going to show him how we always think of others by giving them a new home. We were going to show him that *we* are the ones who spread cheer and the Klauses only spread fear."

"You're telling me that you thought *stealing penguins* was the right thing to do?" Dad said frostily.

Maybe we hadn't quite thought it through. But our efforts to spread cheer had always worked in the past and Archer's plan was so simple and I thought we had Christmas spirit on our side and . . . I guess not, no,' I said humbly.

Archer tried to explain. "The editor would've had no idea how unhappy the penguins were unless we saved them and gave them a proper home. We were going to show him that all the Klauses cared about was themselves, but you guys – the Christmas Carrolls – you always put other people's needs before your own. We thought it would impress him. We thought it would show him that you really are the most festive family."

"We did it all for you, Dad," I insisted. "We were trying to cheer you up."

"What would have cheered me up was spending time with my family, fixing all that mess at our house," Dad said, his snowshine smile hidden behind stormy eyes. "Or decorating a tree together. Or just knowing my daughter was safe and sound at home."

"I know, but –"

"Is this what all of the Halloween nonsense has done to you?" Dad said. "Has it turned you into someone that creeps around and tricks people? Has all of the darkness and spookiness made you forget about the importance of spreading cheer?"

"No!" I yelled, realising I hadn't even thought about

Halloween and that I'd missed out on *another* evening making spooky decorations with Alice and Liena. "I've been trying to do what you taught me!"

"I haven't taught you to lie and steal and cheat your way into winning competitions, young lady," Dad bellowed. "That goes against everything we believe in."

"But, Dad, I –"

"I can't talk about this any more," Dad said. "If you think you're going to that awful Halloween Haunt after the stunts you pulled tonight, you can think again."

I threw my arms in the air. "I haven't even had the *chance* to do anything Halloweeny!" I yelled, waking Ivy from her sleep and making Reggie jump. "So how could it possibly have changed me? You don't let me *do* anything or *go* anywhere if it isn't to do with this stupid competition. I tried to tell you that I was getting sick of it all, but you ignored me. You were so busy thinking of ways to out-Christmas the Klauses that you didn't even see how upset I was. All I wanted to do was go to *one* sleepover at Alice's house. Just one! Or help make signs for the Halloween Haunt because everyone says I've got the best art and craft skills in the class. Or go skateboarding with Archer so I didn't have to think about Christmas, or Halloween, or anything else for that matter!"

"I don't think shouting is going to help anyone right now, Holly," Mum interrupted. "Let's just get home and have a good night's sleep and we can talk again in the morning. Nick, maybe you can make some winterberry waffles for everyone? Maybe we can record a new Christmas song to raise the festiveness, or sew some special stockings to boost our cheer-o-meters?"

Typical Mum. Any hint of a raised voice or disagreement and she smothered us in Christmas.

I could see right through her. Throwing more Christmas at me wasn't going to make me feel any better. Forcing me to stay at home and sing carols at sunrise wouldn't suddenly put a smile on my face. And feeding me Christmas food and filling my time with Christmas crafts wouldn't help us win the Most Festive Family competition.

"You do know the Klauses will have their house back to normal by morning, don't you?" I said. "They've probably got a team of people fixing the ice rink and snow fountains right now."

Dad let out a long, exaggerated sigh. "Then what do you want to do, Hols? Do you want to help rebuild our home, or do you want to have fun with your friends and forget about the competition?"

The Klauses were going to win the competition, so why were Mum and Dad still trying to compete? The Klauses might not have their dancing penguins any more, but they had everything else. I struggled to find the right words.

"What would you do?" I asked Archer, unable to choose between family and friends, Christmas and Halloween, making my parents happy and making myself happy.

"Skateboarding and sleepovers will always be there, but the editor's visit is just a few days away," Archer said. "Why don't you spend the next few days helping your mum and dad, and then we can have a pizza night or something once it's over? Then everyone's happy."

Happy? HAPPY? Had anyone stopped to think if *I* was happy? Mum and Dad were happy as long as they impressed the editor. Ivy was happy if she got enough sleep. Archer was happy if he spent time with his friends. Reggie was happy as long as he was the centre of attention. Sue was happy when she was cosy and warm. Even the Klauses had found true happiness after tonight.

And then there was me. The one who wasn't allowed an opinion. The one that couldn't do anything she wanted. The one that had to go along with whatever her parents told her in the name of spreading cheer.

"I know it doesn't sound fair," Archer said as we pulled into our dark drive. "But it's the right thing to do."

I rolled my eyes and stepped out of the car. I had no choice, as usual.

"Fine," I huffed. "Let's just get this competition over with."

A FROSTY WELCOME

43

Who knew you could get so much done in four days? Admittedly, everything still looked half finished by the time Saturday rolled around, but considering the fact that Mum had hourly meltdowns, Dad was a bag of nerves and we didn't stop arguing all week, I think we did OK.

I spent the whole of Saturday morning (reluctantly) setting the table for lunch, yawning while I redecorated my broken hobby trees and helping Archer paint a welcome sign for the editor. I probably would've complained more, but because I'd decided to give everyone the silent treatment, it meant I didn't have to listen to their stupid competition countdowns, help Dad fix the lights on the roof, or help Mum make the ninth set of new curtains for the house.

Mum was especially proud of these curtains because she'd designed the fabric herself. She called it her Festive Family Fabric, and it included all the elements of Christmas we loved. She'd turned Ivy's handprint into a Christmas tree and added a tiny star on top. She'd dipped Reggie's hoof in ink and added a drawing of a reindeer I made when I was about six years old. The fabric included little sprigs of holly and ivy, tiny silver snowflakes, a bright red Santa hat, smiley gingerbread biscuits, and even a line from one of the Christmas carols Archer had written. Mum had stayed up every night to print the material, and when she had enough, she made more items of clothing than I'd ever thought possible.

There were matching tops and trousers for all of us, plus socks, slippers, hats and a tiny babygrow for Ivy. Mum made herself an apron, a tea cosy, oven gloves, and cushions for the living room. She also made matching chair covers for the dining room, a tablecloth and napkins, and even a top for Reggie. It was a bit headache-inducing, if I'm honest, but Mum clearly liked the Santa-has-puked-all-over-the-house look, so who was I to argue?

It was almost enough to forget how Christmassy the Klauses' house was. It was *almost* enough to overlook our constant squabbling. It was ALMOST enough to believe we actually had a shot at winning. Almost . . .

DING DONG.

OK, so it wasn't really a 'ding dong'. It was more of a 'jingle bells, jingle bells, jingle all the way' (fourteen times in a row), but I'd be here all day if I wrote that out.

The editor of *The Christmas Chronicle* arrived at two o'clock on the dot. He was a small, middle-aged man with a round tummy and a warm smile that made his eyes crinkle.

"WELCOME!" Dad shouted, running out of the kitchen with two pans and a jug of milk. "I'm just putting the finishing touches to lunch. Make yourself at home."

"SNOW WONDERFUL TO MEET YOU!" Mum beamed, rushing to give the editor one of her infamous yeti hugs. "Would you like a drink? We had planned to offer you twelve different flavours of eggnog, have a make-your-own hot chocolate station, and share our special cinnamon water recipe after lunch, but we've been a bit, umm . . . preoccupied." She gulped. "Someone – we won't name names – tried to –"

"Snow!" Dad snapped, wrapping his arm around Mum and almost accidentally knocking her out with a saucepan. "Remember we said we wouldn't mention what happened this week? We don't need to stoop to their level."

Mum bit her lip and nodded.

"I admit, we've had a tricky week," Dad said, beaming his snowshine smile at the editor. "But no one can take the Carrolls' cheer away. No, ho, ho!"

I rolled my eyes. Could Dad be any more fake right

now? We hadn't exactly been cheerful when we were arguing about how many Christmas crafts I could fit in after school. Why, then, was he acting like everything was snowtacularly perfect?

The editor smiled. "Glad to hear it. I –"

BEEP BEEP. BEEP BEEP.

"Argh!" Dad yelled, sending Mum flying as he sprinted back into the kitchen. "My cheertatoes!"

The editor pushed his round glasses up his nose. "Shall we wait for him to come back?" he said. "Or would you like to give me a house tour now?"

"Now," I said grumpily. "Let's just get it out the way."

"Out the way?" the editor said, pulling a notepad and pen from the pocket of his crisp corduroy blazer. "Very well. Why don't you start by telling me what Christmas Day is like for the Carrolls. What do you normally do first?"

Mum shot me a look that said, 'I know you're annoyed at us but we won't be rushed, young lady', and then she began the longest description EVER of a dreamlike, perfect Christmas that would probably out-Christmas Santa himself.

"Well!" she said with a clap, guiding the editor past the embarrassing Christmas calendar I'd made when I was four and the wonky photos from Christmas pasts that hung along the stairs. "First, we sing carols on the lawn and wish the neighbours a Merry Christmas. Some of our favourite carols include —"

"I'm sure the editor doesn't need to know every little thing, Mum," I said, trailing grumpily behind them.

"Then we eat breakfast," Mum continued, her voice getting more high-pitched to drown out the clattering in the kitchen and my I-hope-you-know-how-annoyed-I-am sighs. "Breakfast always consists of the three berries: winterberry waffles in the shape of snowflakes or sleighs, bowls of Santaberries with whipped cream beards and Santa hats, and cloudberry jam on toast for Ivy. We have different bowls and cups for each one, and we normally –"

"We'll be here all day at this rate, Mum," I hissed. "Can't you just email him our ice-tinerary?"

Mum hurried the editor past Dad's home-made ice lanterns and acted like she hadn't heard me at all. Wow. Putting on a fake, squealy voice. Trying to portray us as the perfect family. Ignoring her children. Who did that remind me of?

"And then we open our stockings by the fire," Mum continued, walking into the living room to show off her curtains and cushions and Ivy's collection of elf teddy bears. "Then we walk around the village to post notes of cheer and merry wishes, take a trip to the food bank to donate food and the Christmas jumpers we've made, visit the care home to give them some home-made socks and grotto cakes, get back for lunch and games, make phone calls to family and friends, exchange presents and make Christmas Day ornaments for the tree."

The editor pursed his lips as he scrambled to write everything down. "And you do that all in one day?" he said.

"Oh no," Mum said, fiddling with her giant Santa hat earrings. "We do that every day."

The editor practically choked on air. "*Every day? How do you have time for anything else?*"

I scoffed. "We don't."

"There's always time to spread cheer!" Mum practically yelled so he didn't hear me. "Don't you think?"

The editor scribbled something else in his notebook and turned to look at the ceiling, which was covered in hundreds of Christmas cards and gift tags with kind messages and notes of cheer.

"OOOOOOOOOWWWW!" Dad yelled desperately from the kitchen. "SNOW! Could you come here a moment? I need a little elfsistance."

Mum did an awkward curtsey-bow-hug thing to the editor. "Nothing to worry about!" she sang as she ran out of the room. "Why don't you all make your way to the dining room? Lunch will be ready in a jingle-bell jiffy and then we can play some games!"

Archer was already in the dining room when we arrived. "Holly," he said, waving me to the corner of the room. "You know I need to leave in a couple of hours, don't you? For the Halloween Haunt?"

My heart sank. "I know," I said, glancing out of the window. "I wish I could go with you."

THE CHRISTMAS REHEARSAL

44

"I am SO sorry about the turkey," Dad said, sweating as he placed the blackened bird in the middle of the table. "This has never happened before. It's a new oven, you see. I haven't had a proper chance to test it. Must've set the wrong temperature. Or the alarm is broken."

"It's quite all right," the editor said, pulling a chair out and taking his seat.

SQUELCH.

With a mixture of shock and confusion on his face, the editor jumped out of his chair and peeled a wet piece of paper away from his trousers.

"Oh dear!" Dad cried, waving his hands like there was some sort of elfmergency. "Oh deer, oh deer, oh reindeer."

"Our welcome sign!" Archer said. "We were leaving it there to dry. I'm so sorry!"

I would've been sorry, too, if I hadn't found the whole thing so amusing. Maybe now the editor would go home. Maybe he'd come back another day and I could sneak away to the Halloween Haunt with Archer. Maybe, just maybe, we'd all get what we wanted? I felt my cheer-o-meter rating rise a point or two, but it lasted about two seconds before it plummeted to a measly minus five again.

"Don't worry," Mum said, pulling the editor in the direction of her studio. "I've got just the thing!"

The editor reappeared five minutes later, wearing what looked like every single thing Mum had ever made.

"I've given him some Festive Family Fabric trousers," Mum said, looking at the editor like she was his proud mother on the first day of school. "But I'd completely forgotten about the snowtacular fluffy jumper I'd already made him! And the apron that says 'There's snow Christmas like Christmas with the Carrolls!'. AND the bobble hat that plays *We Wish You A Merry Christmas* every hour, on the hour. It's quite christmariffic, don't you think?"

"It's very, umm . . ." The editor looked at his feet, which were covered in Festive Family Fabric socks and matching slippers. "Extravagant."

Mum beamed. "Thank you. Now, shall we eat?"

Dad popped a towel on the editor's seat so he didn't sit in any of the spilled paint left over from the welcome-sign disaster. "Crackers first!" he declared with excitement. "Always crackers first. And this year, I've been working on an extra special cracker. The World's Largest Christmas Cracker, to be precise!" He ran out of the room and came back pushing a giant cracker on a wheelbarrow.

"I thought you asked *me* to make the World's Largest Christmas Cracker?" I said, forgetting all about my no-talking-to-Dad-rule.

"I know, Snowflake," Dad said. "But you said it was all getting a bit much."

The editor raised his eyebrows.

"What he means," Mum said, plonking a Festive Family Fabric hat on her head, "is that Holly was finding everything so winterful and christastic and snowperb, she needed a little lie-down. Didn't you, Snowdrop?"

"Not exactly," I said, wondering when my parents had turned into such fibbers. "I just wanted a break from Christmas. I wanted to go to the Halloween Hau–"

"LET'S PULL THIS CRACKER!" Dad's voice boomed around the room. "GATHER ROUND, GATHER ROUND."

Dad and the editor held one end of the cracker, while Mum, Archer and I (reluctantly) grabbed the other.

"OK, everyone," said Dad. "Three. Two. One . . ."

THE FAILED FESTIVITIES

45

What happened next sounds like an elaborate joke or a horror movie or one of those lies that grow and grow and grow until you don't even remember what you were lying about in the first place. But I promise you, this is absnowlutely true.

What Dad had failed to tell us about the World's Largest Christmas Cracker, was that he'd invented the world's biggest indoor firework and hidden it inside. It was a mix between a whizzing, fizzing firecracker that goes *BANG!* when it explodes and an enormous hand-held sparkler. Dad had *also* failed to tell us that he hadn't had time to test it. So when we pulled it and the indoor firework whizzed and fizzed and sparked and banged, the explosion was ~~a little~~ a lot bigger than expected. In fact, the sparks were so big, they flew on to Mum's new Festive Family Fabric tablecloth and set the whole table alight.

"My table!" Mum yelled.

"The turkey!" Dad cried. "I can't burn the turkey *twice*!"

Archer grabbed a jug of Dad's new Festiwater and poured it over the table. It doused the flames immediately, but left the cheertatoes floating in a sea of sparkly liquid.

We stood in silence for a few moments.

Nobody knew what to do next.

"Shall we reschedule?" I said eventually, feeling the cheeriest I had all day. "I want to go to the Halloween Haunt with Archer anyway. I know I've been banned and everything, but if I go with Archer, Dad can spend some time getting to know the new oven and Mum can make some Festive Family Fabric underwear to go with the tops, trousers, aprons, socks, slippers and hats. I'm sure you'd want to see that."

"For the last time, Holly, you're not going to the Halloween Haunt," Dad snapped, using his tinsel tongs to fish cheertatoes out of the Festiwater.

"And I'm on a rather tight deadline," the editor added. "I'm here today and at the Klauses tomorrow. That's all I have time for I'm afraid."

"Don't you think it's a bit unfair the Klauses get a whole extra day to prepare?" I said, watching Dad's temple pulsate. "Not that it would make a difference anyway, because they've got the fanciest, Christmassiest, most impressively impressive house you could dream of."

"That's enough, Hols," Dad barked, grabbing some home-made Christmas hats from a drawer at the side. "We've got so many things to talk to you about, Mr Editor, but the Klauses aren't one of them."

"So, er, what other traditions do you have?" the editor said, trying his best to get back on track.

"Well, we're only allowed to wear red or green," I said, counting the traditions on my fingers. "We only listen to Christmas carols in the car. We eat nothing but roast dinners and drink hot chocolate, even in the height of summer. I'm not allowed to do anything for myself if I don't spread cheer to others and –"

"Ho, ho, ho!" Dad laughed, holding his belly like a bowl full of jelly. "Holly is just joking, of course. Everyone knows you can't spread cheer unless you're cheerful yourself." He gave me an unusually stern glare that made me feel like the World's Largest Christmas Cracker ready to explode.

"But I'm not cheerful!" I yelled. Archer awkwardly slipped down in his seat. "I've been telling you for weeks that I'm not cheerful. And all you did was make me feel bad that I wasn't helping prepare for today."

"Today was a big deal for us," Dad said, still trying to smile through the awkwardness.

"Well, look what's happened!" I cried. "You've forced me to stay here and everything's turning into a chrisaster!"

"It's only a chrisaster because you're making it one," Mum whispered out of the corner of her mouth.

"I don't know why you're putting on this perfect

family act," I said, nowhere near finished with my rant. "You're as bad as the Klauses!"

The festadio, which must've got caught in the indoor-firework-Festiwater-explosion, screeched to a halt. So Mum, of course, felt like she had to fill the silence.

"Siiiiilent night," she sang in a tone that sounded like a choking cat. "Hoooooly night. ALL IS CAAAAALM. ALL IS BRIIII–"

"I can't believe you're doing this, Holly," Dad said, forcefully piling more twice-burnt turkey on to the editor's plate. "You knew how much today meant to us."

"And you knew how much the Halloween Haunt meant to me!"

"HALLOWEEN!" Dad bawled. "The night everyone forgets about spreading cheer and spreads fear instead? You don't understand –"

"No, YOU don't understand!" I yelled. "I should be able to make my own mind up about something. Just because you and Mum don't like Halloween, it doesn't mean I won't. Just because you didn't have any friends and spent all your time finding joy in Christmas doesn't mean the same thing is going to happen to me."

"Siiiiilent night," Mum continued, getting louder. "Hoooooly night. Shepherds quaaaake AT THE SIIIIGHT."

I wasn't finished. "I actually have friends, Dad. I have Archer and Alice and Liena and the other kids at school. I've even made friends with Setti and Toby Klaus."

Dad's mouth dropped open.

"Yes. Really! Making friends isn't that hard. It's not about spreading cheer or giving gifts. It's about just being yourself! Not that you and Mum will know much about that, of course. You've been too busy speaking in posh accents and trying to impress the Klauses to remember what's really important."

"SLEEP IN HEAVENLY PEEEEEACE, OH, SLEEEEEP IN HEEEEAVENLY PEACE . . ."

"I want you to have friends, Holly!" Dad exclaimed, sliding the whole blackened turkey on the editor's plate. "But I want you to be friends with us, too!"

JINGLE BELLS. JINGLE BELLS . . . went the front

door bell.

WHAT NOW?

"That'll be the photographer," the editor said, raising his hand as if he was too afraid to speak.

Archer had barely opened the door when the photographer ran inside, chased by Reggie hee-hawing at the top of his lungs.

"ARRRRGH!" the photographer shouted, hurtling into the dining room and cowering behind the editor's chair. "Get your dog off me!"

Fixated on the photographer's camera, Reggie ran in too – but slipped on the puddle of Festiwater on the floor and landed on the table. Christmas tree number fifteen crashed down on the table too and sent food flying in all directions.

"Heeee-haaaaaaw!" Reggie yelled, trying to pose for the camera lens.

Mashed cheertatoes splattered across the walls. Dad put his hands on his head. Mum stopped singing, Archer tried to save Reggie – and Ivy projectile-vomited her dinner all over the editor's head.

Click. FLASH. "How many photos you want me to take, boss?" said the photographer.

The editor wiped chewed-up carrot out of his eyes and pushed a puddle of gravy off his lap.

"Thank you, Carrolls," he said, chucking his ruined notepad in the bin. "I think I've seen enough."

THE MEMORY BOOK

46

N one of us moved for several minutes after the editor and photographer had left.

The Klauses hadn't needed to wreck our home or take our cheer away or ruin our chance of winning the competition. We had done all that ourselves.

The ho-ho clock struck three o'clock. A glimmer of hope ignited inside me. I know I was banned from the Halloween Haunt, but *technically* I could still make it if I could make Dad change his mind. All I needed was to make myself a mask, fashionise an outfit that wasn't red or green, and get to school in time for the party. But . . . did I actually want to go now?

Mum looked the saddest I had ever seen her. Dad looked like he was about to throw up. Even Reggie sat in the corner with a guilty expression on his face. How could I go and have fun at a party when I'd just ruined what could have been one of the most exciting days of Mum and Dad's lives?

I groaned quietly. The Klauses were right. I didn't even deserve a lump of coal in my stocking. Over the last two weeks I'd tricked, lied, trespassed, kidnapped penguins and spread about as much cheer as a truckload of reindeer poop. What had happened to me? I used to be so cheery. So carefree. So –

"Ho, ho," Dad chuckled to himself. "Ho, ho, ho."

I looked up. "Dad?" I said. "What's so funny?"

"Ho, ho, ho," Dad laughed louder, his shoulders shaking. "HO, HO, HO, HO, HO!"

Another giggle came from across the room. It was Mum. She wasn't whimpering any more. In fact, a smile crept across her face and she was soon laughing, too. Archer was next, followed by Reggie, whose loud hee-haws almost drowned out Dad. They all laughed harder and harder and harder until tears streamed down their faces and they could barely catch their breath.

Then something strange happened. A bubble of laughter rose in my own throat. It forced the edges of my mouth to rise and made my eyes water. Within seconds, I was laughing, too. I wasn't even sure why.

"What a day!" Dad bawled, almost doubled over. "I *burned* the turkey! Can you believe it?"

"And the festadio broke!" Mum cried, using a napkin to wipe her cheeks.

"The tree fell down! The decorations smashed!"

"Ivy threw up over the editor!" Mum howled.

"He couldn't . . ." Dad could barely get his words out. "He couldn't even write anything down in his notebook," he squeaked. "It was drenched!"

"And the photographer thought Reggie was a guard dog!" Mum laughed so hard she gave herself hiccups.

"Can you imagine what we'll look like in that photo?"

"Hee-haw, hee-haw, heeeee-haw!" Reggie brayed in delight.

"He sat on your sign!" Dad continued, snorting so loud it made us all laugh twice as hard.

"His bum looked like . . . like . . ." I fell on to the floor, unable to contain myself.

"I didn't even get to give him my memory book," Archer said, pulling it out of his bag and holding it above his head. "What should I do with it now?"

We stared at the book in Archer's hands.

The laughing subsided.

"My dear boy," Dad said. "Can we have a look?"

Five minutes later, we were sitting in front of the flickering fire in the living room. Mum wrapped us in fluffy blankets and Dad laid out a pudding picnic with snowball sundaes, pinecone pies and rainbow wreath cakes that filled the floor.

Archer opened the memory book. On the very first page, he'd drawn a picture of us and written the words: *The Most Festive Family: The Christmas Carrolls.*

"I made it to convince the editor to pick you," Archer said, his cheeks turning red. "Because to me, you *are* the most festive family, and you always will be."

Reggie nodded his head in agreement.

Dad pulled us all in for a hug. "Thank you, Archer," he said. "You don't know how much that means to us."

Each page of Archer's book had a different photo stuck to the paper, with notes written in sparkly pen around the edges.

"This was the sleepover in the stables," Archer said, pointing at a photo of Sue twirling in the air, Reggie leaping off hay bales to practise his flying, and me clapping and singing in the background.

"That was the time we gave Reggie a bath," he said, pointing at a photo of the three of us squeezed around the bath with Reggie proudly showing off his bubble beard. "Then there's some photos of our reindeer costumes at the Klauses' party. It was a strange evening, but it's pretty funny to look back on."

We laughed and pointed at the different photos, occasionally stopping to reminisce about things we'd remembered.

"Your mum gave me this photo of you and your dad sitting in the refreshmas fountain, Holly," Archer explained. "She said she took it through the window when you were having some kind of heart-to-heart."

"We were talking about my childhood," Dad said, squeezing my hand. "I was telling Holly about why I love Christmas so much."

"There are even photos from last week when everyone helped fix the house," Archer said. "See, there's Prisha repainting the front door, Rishi and Esme replanting the trees, and there's Snow and Norman walking around the garden."

I grabbed a corner of the book and looked closer. "Does Norman look familiar to you?" I said, focusing in on his yellow hard hat and bushy moustache.

Mum shrugged her shoulders. "I don't think so, Snowdrop. But we should invite him over for dinner soon. We'd have no working fairy lights or decorations on the roof if it weren't for him!"

I thought about Norman and the other people who had gone out of their way to help put our house back together. They had all left their families or jobs or worries to put smiles back on *our* faces. I should've noticed sooner. I should've realised that these people were doing something good for someone else, and all I could think about was sneaking off to the Klauses'.

We spent the next hour or so flicking through Archer's memory book. We told stories about finding penguins in the school kitchen and finally seeing Reggie fly. We ate Christmas cakes and drank hot chocolate with extra christmallows, and even sang some carols with Reggie providing some super-creative hee-haw harmonies.

Then, something happened that was more surprising than Santa sipping sangria in a swimsuit . . .

REUNITED 46

JINGLE BELLS. JINGLE BELLS . . .

I opened the front door and found myself face to face with a tiny, fluffy, big-footed . . .

"SUE?"

The baby penguin flapped her flippers and raised her beak in the air. "Peep peep!"

"Is it OK that we're here?" Setti said, pulling Sue away from my face and motioning towards the Elfler, who sat in a dark green limousene on the driveway. "Sue wanted to see you."

"What are you doing here?' Archer asked, squeezing into the door frame with Mum, Dad, Ivy and Reggie not far behind.

Toby's mouth twitched nervously. "We shouldn't have been so mean to the penguins," he said, doing an awkward half-wave. "We went to visit them in their new home and they were so happy and relaxed and they only danced when they wanted to. We know now that they should have been there all along."

Christmas cheer soared through me at the thought of Setti and Toby finally putting other people's (or animals') needs before their own.

"They *were* much happier," Setti admitted. "But Sue wasn't. She didn't want to dance or mix with the other penguins at all."

"She didn't?" I said, instantly wanting to check if she was warm enough.

"We think she missed you," Setti said. "All of you."

Reggie let out a quiet 'hee-haw' and Sue returned his cry with a 'peep'.

"We fed and played with the penguins for ages," Toby explained. "But when we tried to leave, Sue wouldn't let us go."

"She kept running after us and pecking our legs," Setti said, rubbing her ankle.

"And then she climbed on to a wall and jumped into the boot of our limo all by herself! It was like she'd done it before."

I grinned. "She's a bit stubborn," I said.

"And she's an expert escape artist!" Archer laughed.

Sue let out a proud 'peep' and waddled towards us. First, she wrapped her flippers around my ankle and then she stared at Reggie until Dad lifted her up and nestled her between Reggie's ears.

"So what does this mean?" Mum said, letting Ivy stroke Sue's slippery feathers.

"It means we have another member of the family," I said, my tummy bubbling with an ~~excited fart~~ exifart. I shot Mum and Dad the biggest, happiest, hopefullest snowshine smile I could muster. "Right?"

"Of course!" Mum cried. "With the right paperwork and approval of course. Welcome to the family, Sue. Shall I make you a blanket to keep you warm at night?

I'm sure I've got some spare Festive Family Fabric somewhere."

We huddled around Sue and talked about all the adventures we'd have with a diva ~~donkey~~ reindeer, a dancing penguin and our new best friends, Setti and Toby.

"I think you're all forgetting something," Dad said a few minutes later.

The room fell silent. Sue hid behind Reggie's ear. What was he going to say? That Sue couldn't stay with us? That she had to stay in the zoo? Or go back to the Klauses?

"You're going to be late for the Halloween Haunt," Dad said, a warm smile stretching across his face.

It took a moment for my brain to register what he had said.

"The Halloween Haunt?" I repeated. "You're . . . letting me go?"

Dad nodded. "I'm sorry, Snowflake. This whole competition clouded my judgement. I let my competitiveness get the better of me. Your mum and

I – we've never understood Halloween. And after the Hallomas party and what we thought was a huge Halloween prank when the house got ruined, I was worried you might get swept up in it all. I thought you might not enjoy Christmas any more. I thought you wouldn't want to spend time with us. I thought I'd lose my little girl."

"You could never lose me, Dad," I said, wrapping my arms around his soft belly as the smell of peppermint and chocolate surrounded me. "But people change."

I watched Setti and Toby tickle Sue's head and take photos of Reggie on their camera phones. And Archer, who had once been so nervous about standing out, playing peekaboo with Ivy and singing a Christmas carol at the top of his lungs.

"Change can be scary," I said, looking up at Dad. "But it can also be good. Me celebrating Halloween doesn't mean I won't love you any more. And it doesn't mean I'll stop celebrating Christmas. It just means I'm becoming my own person. It means I'm learning to be myself."

Dad hugged me a little tighter. "When did you get so wise?" he said, ruffling my hair.

Setti checked the time on her shiny new phone and grabbed Toby's hand. "We have to go now," she said reluctantly.

"Yeah, but thanks for having us," added Toby.

Dad joined in with Archer's carol as Setti and Toby climbed into their limo. Toby took one final photo of Reggie from the window and Mum handed them some mince pies for the road.

"I suppose you've got a lot to do before the editor of *The Christmas Chronicle* visits you tomorrow?" she asked.

"Actually," Setti said, smiling from ear to ear. "Mother and Father said we could have a games night tonight. They've cancelled all of their plans so we can make puzzles, play Monopoly and then have races on the toboggan track. The winner gets a golden sleigh and everything!"

"A golden sleigh?" Toby groaned. "Father told me it was going to be made from diamonds."

"Does it matter?" Setti replied. "You know I'm going to win it anyway. I've already made room for it in my dressing room."

"Nuh-uh," Toby wagged his finger. "It's going in my bedroom."

Setti pursed her lips and thought for a moment. "Why don't we put it in the playroom?" she said. "Then we can share it with Holly and Archer when they come round? It can be like our secret den."

It didn't take long for a huge smile to spread across

Toby's face. "Deal."

An hour later, Archer and I arrived at the Halloween Haunt. We hadn't had time to make new outfits or collect Archer's costume from his house, so we made do with what we had.

That's right! The connected reindeer costumes were back!

Mum had added some cobwebs to the antlers and painted our faces grey so we looked like reindeer zombies. We didn't look as festive or sparkly as I would've liked, but I enjoyed myself anyway. The party wasn't even that scary, and Miss Eversley let me bring the spare sweets home from the trick-or-treat bowls so we could wrap them up as little gifts for the children down the street. It was a good compromise: doing something non-Christmassy but still spreading cheer. It was where I felt most comfortable. I wanted to have fun and try new things, but I also wanted to spread cheer to others. I guess that's where I found the most cheer myself.

The rest of the week felt pretty normal. Dad spent every evening in the kitchen, proving to himself that he *could* cook the perfect turkey. Mum had some lessons to improve her carol-singing, and I even went to Alice's house for a sleepover (although I was looking forward to helping Mum make Festive Family Fabric dressing gowns when I got home).

All in all, I thought things turned out OK. We weren't going to win the Most Festive Family competition, but I didn't mind that. I had the most cheer-spreading, hilarious, caring parents in the world. I had the bestest best friend anyone could wish for. I had a real flying diva ~~donkey~~ reindeer who was protective and loyal, and a baby penguin who was the best dancer I had ever seen. I had a baby sister who was so clever, she was the first to notice anything strange or unusual (she also had great aim when it came to projectile-vomiting on people!). And I had learned that the best way to spread cheer was to be cheerful myself.

That's right. You couldn't just *pretend* to be cheerful.

It came across as fake and forced and people could see it a mile off – like Mr Klaus's blinding-white teeth. That's why it was so important to do things you loved. That's why it was important to surround yourself with people you cared about and people that cared about you. That's why it was important to find laughter even in the middle of a chrisaster. If *you* were cheerful, the cheer would spread to others.

And that's all there was to it.

THE CHRISTMAS CHRONICLE

47

Archer arrived at the same time as the post a couple of days later. We were all huddled in the kitchen in our Festive Family Fabric dressing gowns and Dad was scooping batter into a pan to make us some winterberry waffles.

"So what are you two doing today?" Mum said, sorting through the letters the postie had just delivered. "Are you going skateboarding again?"

"I think so," I said, as Archer played peekaboo with Reggie and Sue outside the window. "But then I think I'll make a start on this year's hobby tree."

"Oh?" Dad said, his eyes lighting up. "And what will your hobby be this year?"

"I was thinking of a skateboarding tree," I said. "With tinsel stuck to the edges of the skateboards, lights in the wheels, and –"

"AAHHHHHHHHH!" Mum squealed.

Archer jumped out of his skin. Dad dropped his batter on the floor. Ivy stared at Mum, unsure whether to cry or not.

"No," Mum said, her face turning grey. "No, no, no, no, no, no, no."

"What is it?" I said in alarm. "What's wrong?"

Mum slowly pushed the stack of unopened letters to the side. At the very bottom of the pile was a copy of *The Christmas Chronicle*. And there, on the front cover, was a photo of us, our broken Christmas table and Reggie showcasing his cheesiest, wonkiest, happiest grin.

And across the top in shiny red letters were the words:

Meet the Christmas Carrolls – WINNERS of the Most Festive Family competition.

I am thrilled to announce this year's winners of the Most Festive Family competition are the Carrolls, also affectionately and appropriately known as the Christmas Carrolls, of Sleigh Ride Avenue.

The Carrolls believe in spreading cheer throughout the year. Not only do they do this by giving to charity and doing things for others, they do this by just being themselves. They are abundantly jolly, endearingly eccentric, but also entirely normal.

Despite some stiff competition from the Klauses of Candy Cane Lane, who wowed me with a twelve-course meal, a private showing of **The Nutcracker** *ballet, and a tour of their Klausland theme park, the Carrolls created the kind of Christmas we can all relate to.*

The Christmas rehearsal I witnessed at the Carrolls' was messy, chaotic, hilarious, loud, and, truth be told, a bit of a let-down. But that, my festive readers, is exactly why they won! I'm sure we can all relate to a Christmas filled with disagreements, burned turkey, soggy potatoes, incidents with beloved pets and falling

Christmas trees, out-of-tune singing from a drunk relative who insists on starting karaoke before you've had dessert, and even being forced to wear matching Christmas jumpers that belong in the seventies.

The Carrolls bake deliciously creative Christmas treats, make all of their own presents and use hand-made decorations on their trees. But these things weren't what impressed me most. What impressed me was that despite all their efforts to put on the most extravagant Christmas possible, they had a day like any other. A day filled with smiles and tantrums. A day filled with joyful memories and frustrating setbacks. A day filled with laughter and shock and disappointment, which is what makes Christmas so wonderfully memorable.

This wasn't the only reason I chose the Carrolls to win this competition. Oh no. My favourite kind of journalism is investigative journalism. I like to go undercover and really experience what I'm writing about. And this is exactly what I did with the Klauses and the Carrolls.

First, I went undercover at the Klauses' as a security guard. I saw just how much effort went into the upkeep of Candy Cane Lane and their dedication to creating the perfect Christmas. But then I went to the Carrolls', and I helped them rebuild their home after it was mysteriously destroyed a few days before their Christmas rehearsal. And even though the Carrolls had barely any time to fix their broken decorations or one-of-a-kind inventions, they still had time for everyone else. They still had time for me. Nick Carroll made us treats from his kitchen. Snow Carroll asked me about my family and my job, and even invited me and my family back to meet their reindeer.

If you haven't already guessed, the Carrolls embody the true meaning of Christmas. They are caring, selfless, quirky, friendly and they really do spread cheer all year. And that is why I'm delighted to announce they ARE the Most Festive Family.

Congratulations, Carrolls.

We were all too bumfuzzled to know what to say.

"So . . . the editor was NORMAN?" I said at last. "The man with the yellow hat and bushy moustache that helped put the house back together?"

"I had no idea!" Mum gasped. "He looked so different when he came to visit us as the editor of *The Christmas Chronicle*. He'd shaved his moustache. He'd combed his hair. He wore a fancy corduroy blazer."

"And he was the original security elf-ficer at the Klauses' house?" Archer said, trying to lift Reggie and Sue through the window because they didn't want to miss out on any of the excitement.

"That's why he wasn't there when we went back to free the penguins," I said slowly. "He'd gone back to his job at *The Christmas Chronicle*. It all makes sense now."

"Oh, how rude of us, Nick!" Mum cried. "We were so busy trying to impress him during the rehearsal, we didn't ask his name or even what he wanted for Christmas! What must he think of us?"

"Never mind that," Dad said, reading the rest of the

article. "We won! We actually won! Do you realise what that means?"

A spark of a memory made my heart beat in double-time.

"The parade?" I squealed. "We're going to be in the Christmas Season Parade?"

Dad turned the magazine pages towards us. "We need to get packing," he said, shooting us the biggest snowshine smile I've ever seen. "We're going to New York City for Christmas!"

THE END

COMING SOON!

THE CHRISTMAS CARROLLS

3

Holly's DICTIONARY

PAGE	HOLLY'S WORD	WHAT SHE MEANS
3, 157, 315, 337	Fashionise	A made-up word
4, 6, 242, 245	Decorventions	A made-up word
5	Imprealous	A made-up word
8	Baubilliant	A made-up word
17, 18	Explite/Explitement	A made-up word
19, 280	Undubidedly	Undoubtedly
19	Bakeventions	A made-up word
26	Disgustament	A made-up word
54	Fartyness	A made-up word
58	Sasspiciously	Suspiciously
64	Cheerutation	A made-up word
68	Unnervitating	A made-up word
87	Instantizzy	A made-up word
108	Fudgement	Judgement
132, 320	Fashionise	A made-up word
152, 168	Frantical	A made-up word
214	Snortaughing	A made-up word
215	Snortaughee	A made-up word
262	Nelfjas	A made-up word
274	Worhaustion	A made-up word
278, 281	Exifarts	A made-up word

REAL MEANING

To make high-fashion clothes out of everyday items

Decoration inventions

When you're so impressed, you're jealous

A mix between bauble and brilliant!

Exploding with excitement

When you're 100% certain about something

Baking inventions

When you're disgusted and disappointed at the same time

A tardy fart (when a fart slips out later than expected)

When someone acts strangely and you're not sure why

A reputation for being cheerful

A mixture of unnerving and irritating

Instantly dizzy

When your thoughts become thick and sludgy like fudge

To make high-fashion clothes out of everyday items

A mix between being frantic and hysterical

Snorting while you laugh

Snortaughing so hard that a bit of pee comes out!

Elf ninjas

When you're worried and exhausted at the same time

When you're so excited, you accidentally let out a fart

COCOA TEA RECIPE

Feel festive every day of the year with Gram Gram's special cocoa tea recipe. Now, if I'm being totally honest (and I nearly always am), this recipe isn't entirely written by Gram Gram. She won't tell anyone what her secret ingredients are, so I've used my in-ish-ee-ah-tiv to come up with the ingredients that could be in there.

INGREDIENTS *(that I'm pretty sure are in there):*
- Chocolate balls (these are raw chocolate balls that come from Jamaica, which is where Dad is from)
- Cinnamon sticks
- Nutmeg
- Milk
- Bay leaves

INGREDIENTS *(that I think / hope / would like to be in there):*
- Popping candy
- A dash of sugary peppermint from a melted candy cane
- Honey
- Marshmallows
- Whipped cream
- Chocolate sprinkles

And most importantly, the ingredient I know is definitely, one hundred per cent, totally, unquestionably in there because it's the ingredient that adds all the flavour and festive fizziness . . . a HUGE dollop of Christmas cheer.

INSTRUCTIONS:

This is one big ~~experiment~~ elf-speriment because I have no idea how much of each ingredient to use. I'm going with a the-more-sugary-the-better approach, but as long as the chocolate has fully melted into the milk, I'm sure it'll be merrylicious.

STEP 1: Pop a cinnamon stick and a bay leaf into boiling water (this is the only stage Dad will tell me, and while I'm not sure how a stick and a leaf will make cocoa tea, it makes the kitchen smell nice as it simmers for around fifteen minutes, and it makes me feel like a proper chef!).

STEP 2: Grate the chocolate balls into a fine powder and then add some grated nutmeg. This will help it dissolve in the water quicker – I assume.

STEP 3: Add the grated chocolate and nutmeg powder to the boiling water. You've probably got time to practise two or three Christmas carols while it dissolves.

STEP 4: Now add some milk to make it super-thick and creamy, and mix, mix, mix, until it has the consistency of melted ice cream.

STEP 5: This is when you might want to add some honey, whipped cream, marshmallows or melted candy canes for extra sweetness.

STEP 6: Once you're happy with how your cocoa tea tastes, pour it through a sieve to remove any lumps and then go crazy with the popping candy and chocolate sprinkles.

STEP 7: Lastly, pour some mugs for your closest friends and family, pop on a Christmas movie, and sip and slurp your cocoa tea until every delicious drop has gone.

12 DAYS OF CHEER CHALLENGE

Tick off one challenge per day and spread cheer all year just like the Christmas Carrolls!

- TELL SOME JOKES TO YOUR FRIENDS OR FAMILY
- RECOMMEND A BOOK OR FILM YOU ENJOYED
- LITTER PICK AT SCHOOL OR IN YOUR LOCAL AREA
- SING A CHRISTMAS CAROL (OR INVENT YOUR OWN!)
- TAKE PART IN A CHRISTMAS QUIZ
- GIVE AT LEAST ONE PERSON A COMPLIMENT
- WRITE A CARD TO SOMEONE YOU'RE THANKFUL FOR
- HAVE A 10-MINUTE DANCE PARTY!
- WEAR SOMETHING THAT MAKES YOU SMILE
- OFFER TO HELP AT HOME OR AT SCHOOL
- PLAY A GAME WITH YOUR ENTIRE CLASS
- MAKE SOMEONE A HANDMADE DECORATION

Check out the Carrolls' first adventure!

'A CHRISTMAS BOOK ABOUT KINDNESS AND CHEER TO MAKE EVEN SCROOGE'S HEART MELT' DAME JACQUELINE WILSON

THE
CHRISTMAS CARROLLS

A FANTASTICALLY FESTIVE FAMILY

MEL TAYLOR-BESSENT

ILLUSTRATED BY SELOM SUNU

ACKNOWLEDGEMENTS
(Also known as Santa's GOOD LIST)

Hi, everyone.

My name is Archer Edwards (you might know me as Holly's best friend), and I'm here to say thank you to a few people that helped bring this story to life. As you may have seen from the cover, Mel Taylor-Bessent is the author of *The Christmas Carrolls*, but she's busy writing book 3 at the moment, so she's asked me to write these acknowledgements for her.

If you've read the first book in the series, you'll know that I can be a bit shy and I don't always find the right words to say, but in this story (*The Christmas Competition*), I grow in confidence and find my voice, so I think it's only right that I'm the one to shout from the rooftops about how grateful Mel is to the following people . . .

Firstly, to Felicity, who this book is dedicated to. Felicity was Mel's agent and the person who made all her author dreams come true by helping her get *The Christmas Carrolls* published. Although Felicity is following some dreams of her own now, Mel will never forget her kind words, her endless support, her boundless enthusiasm, or her infectious love for Christmas. These books wouldn't exist without Felicity, and we are all eternally grateful to her.

Next, Mel wanted to say an enormous thank you to her new agent, Caroline. In the same way the Carrolls treat me as one of their own, Caroline did the same to Mel and her stories. Mel is so honoured to be represented by Caroline and could not be more excited for the future.

Another giant thank you goes to Mel's publishing team. A bit like how Santa can't fly without his reindeer, Mel can't publish her stories without an incredible team of people pulling her in the right direction. This includes Liz Bankes and Lucy Courtenay (editors), Ryan Hammond (designer), Olivia Carson (marketing), Pippa Poole (publicist), Brogan Furey (sales) and everyone else at Farshore!

Then, of course, there's Mel's mum, who has encouraged Mel's love for writing since she was young. Mel's mum is one of the kindest, most selfless people on the planet, and she is always putting other people before herself. I guess you can see where the Carrolls get some of their traits from!

And then there's Mel's husband, who understands when Mel says she's going to 'spend ten minutes tidying up a chapter', she probably means, 'I'll see you in three hours, can you sort dinner?'. Mel's husband is one of Mel's biggest cheerleaders and has spent most of the last year checking book ratings online, scrolling through comments on social media, and shouting out suggestions when Mel can't think of the right word!

That brings us to Mel's next lot of cheerleaders and cheer spreaders – her friends and family. Mel knows how lucky she is to have found such lifelong friends, and every day really does feel like Christmas when she's with them. In fact, her Christmas wish this year is to spend even more time with them, and to continue writing stories about similar, everlasting friendships. And to Mel's family, who are always so excited to talk about Mel's books and story ideas, thank you for your constant support and kindness, and for purchasing so many copies of *The Christmas Carrolls*, it soared into the bestseller chart!

And of course, this story wouldn't have come to life without the incredible illustrations by Selom Sunu. Mel was blown away by Selom's talent from the moment she saw his sketches of me and Holly, and she could not be more grateful that he agreed to add ~~a little~~ A LOT of magic to the pages of this book. Thank you, Selom, for making us all look so brilliant. I especially love our joined-up reindeer costumes!

OK, I think that's it from . . . oh, Holly just reminded me I need to wish you a Merry Christmas and a Happy New Read. And don't forget to spread cheer, not fear!

Archer

MEL TAYLOR-BESSENT

Founder of the hugely successful Authorfy and Little Star Writing, Mel Taylor-Bessent has made her career connecting readers to their favourite authors and encouraging children to write for pleasure. Now Mel is bringing her own writing to readers with her debut fiction series, *The Christmas Carrolls*.

SELOM SUNU

Selom is a Christian Illustrator and Character Designer who enjoys bringing characters to life visually. Selom has worked on books with KnightsOf and Penguin. He also provides character designs for animation, with Disney TV and CBeebies among his clients.